GHOSTLY

RETURNS

GHOSTLY RETURNS

Stephanie Hansen

For those who believe in magic, never stop. It's all around you if you just look!

BACKGROUND

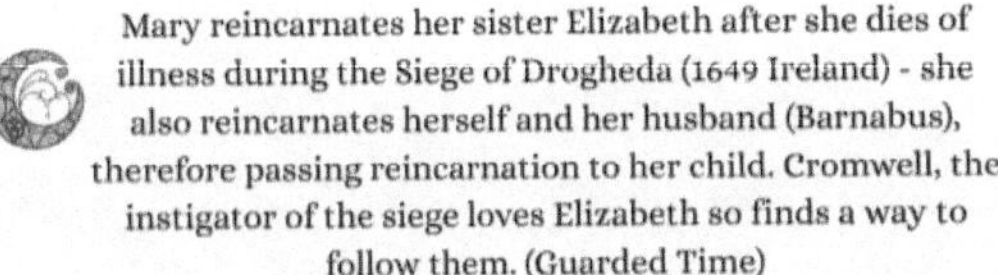

Mary reincarnates her sister Elizabeth after she dies of illness during the Siege of Drogheda (1649 Ireland) - she also reincarnates herself and her husband (Barnabus), therefore passing reincarnation to her child. Cromwell, the instigator of the siege loves Elizabeth so finds a way to follow them. (Guarded Time)

Due to an incident that occurs in the future of their reincarnated souls, Cromwell has sent counters (people created through magic) to fight Marie, Claudia, and Alex (1920). Unfortunately, the soul of his reincarnated love, Anna, pays the price. Marie travels time to try to stop Cromwell at the beginning. Alex & Claudia's love begins here. (Armored Hours)

In our present timeline, many things are occurring. Austria (Claudia's reincarnated soul) needs to stop Cromwell's reincarnated soul from taking over a portal world. She goes to great lengths to do this with her found family and love, Josh, by her side. (Altered Helix) This is also the timeline where a Ghostly Counter world has been created by Cromwell. (Ghostly Howls)

In the future, interplanetary travel is common, and Cromwell has abducted Sierra's dad. She travels to rescue him and finds more sinister things occurring. To save the world, she undergoes an experimental medical procedure. Clones, war, and love (Al) - she finally beats Cromwell by sending telepathic messages that cause him to have a heart attack. Hence, the counters sent to the past as well as the Ghostly Counter world are born. (Transformed Nexus)

Reincarnated Souls Key

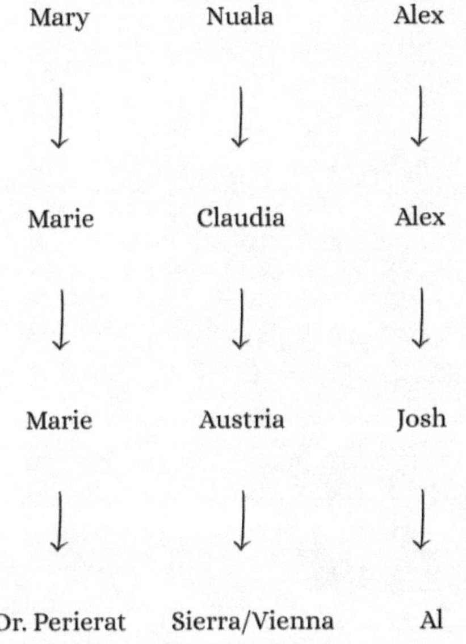

1649 - 1920 - Present - 22ND Century

CHAPTER ONE—MOLLY
"The world is full of magic things, patiently waiting for our senses to grow sharper."
William Butler Yeats

Three years ago, the small town of Ethel, VA, was rocked to its core when the lighthouse became a beacon for something ancient and hungry. Every year since then, we've cast a protection spell, tying knots in rope while visualizing a protective shield, at the weathered tower a week before Samhain, our voices carried away by the salt-tinged wind. This year's no different.

Cormac's slender fingers intertwine with mine as we approach Orla and Dave across the grassy shoreline. We've managed to mostly heal from the toxic tendencies of the past—the jealousy, the competition, the midnight arguments that left scorch marks on the walls. Magical abilities complementing each other have a tendency to do that, like puzzle pieces finally finding their fit.

The mid-October sunlight glints off Cormac's long, blonde hair, turning each strand into spun gold against the blue sky. We don't meet here at night anymore, not since the shadows began to move independently of their owners. She gently squeezes my hand in reassurance, slight crow's feet crinkling around her eyes with a smile that blooms one of my own in return. She tries to continue her broody exterior by wearing a scuffed leather jacket with silver buckles, but her face is too full of light these days to continue the façade.

"It's about time you two showed up," Orla says as she wraps me in a hug, her dark curls tickling my cheek. Her automatic soul-possessing ability takes hold straight away, a warm honey-like sensation flooding through my veins. I feel her anxiety—sharp and metallic—and she feels mine. While hers is about the treacherous events three years ago, mine is about the small velvet box burning a hole in my pocket, holding a moonstone ring for Cormac.

I know she'll say yes; I hear Orla's thoughts echo in my mind like a whisper in an empty room. To assuage her anxiety, I push forward images of Cormac and me from earlier in the morning. We'd stayed in bed, all consumed with passionate kisses and bodies moving in rhythmic dance together; sheets twisted around our ankles, the taste of her still on my lips.

Okay, okay, you're excused for being late, Orla sends through the connection, her mental voice tinged with amusement. Then it's gone as Dave, tall and broad-shouldered in his flannel-lined jacket, gently pulls her out of the hug. He complements her power as Cormac complements mine, his deep voice carrying over the crash of waves against the shore.

"Did you actually expect them to be on time?" he asks her, his breath visible in the chilly air.

Orla looks at me, her eyes sparkling, and we snicker like schoolgirls sharing a secret.

"Some of us know how to keep a woman in bed," I goad Dave, watching his cheeks flush crimson.

Before he can respond, Cormac says, "Guys, I think you should come over here," her voice tight with tension.

She's rounding the other side of the lighthouse, her boots crunching on the path. I jog over to her, worried she might be in danger, the wind whipping my hair across my face. Once I'm next to her, I'm struck with frozen terror, my breath catching in my throat. As Orla and Dave's footsteps catch up, I try to count the sleeping bodies sprinkled around the remnants of a bonfire.

Sprawled across the damp autumn ground lies a peculiar assembly of slumbering figures—some adorned in woolen cloaks and flowing medieval gowns; others draped in shimmering flapper dresses and tweed vests and flat caps. The incongruous sight sends a chill down my spine, conjuring memories of that haunted night years ago when phantoms in pheasant feathers and tarnished armor materialized from the mist. Could history be repeating itself? I draw Cormac closer, my fingers tightening protectively around her shoulder. A bitter wind sweeps through the clearing, rustling crimson leaves and stirring the strange visitors from their dreams.

"Oh, halloo," calls a woman with cascading silver-streaked hair that catches the morning light. Deep laugh lines frame her eyes as she rises gracefully to her feet, brushing debris from her embroidered skirts. Her button nose crinkles above heart-shaped lips as she smiles warmly. "I'm Marie. We weren't expecting anyone so early."

"You're days early for Samhain," Orla informs her, her voice carrying across the clearing.

"Samhain!" exclaims a younger woman with stylish curls and bright eyes. She leaps up, clapping her hands together with enthusiasm, silver bracelets jingling at her wrists. "I'm Florian. I absolutely adore a proper shindig."

Another woman glides forward, her tweed vest firmly hugging her body. She loops her arm possessively around Florian's slender waist and extends her other hand, adorned with bangles that glint in the early light. "Kiersten," she offers, her voice melodic but guarded.

"Molly, and this is Cormac," I reply, mirroring Kiersten's protective gesture by drawing Cormac against my side, feeling her warmth through her leather jacket.

"Might there be lodgings available in your village?" Marie inquires, her eyes scanning the distant rooftops visible through the thinning trees.

"Not anywhere that could accommodate a gathering of this size," Dave responds, his weathered hands resting on his leather belt.

A tall woman with anxious eyes approaches Orla hesitantly. A man with sandy blond hair clutches her trembling arm as she nervously smooths out her skirt. Dave and I don't miss her flinch with his touch, juxtaposing their closeness. It resurfaces memories from when Dave and Orla couldn't touch. "Hello, I'm Claudia," she murmurs, "and may I present Alex?" Her delicate fingers twist together nervously while Alex soothingly rubs her goose-bump-covered arms.

"Orla and Dave," Dave announces, nodding curtly. When Alex extends his hand to Orla, Dave intercedes and shakes his hand, so Orla doesn't have to.

"Um, Orla," Alex interjects, his deep voice surprisingly gentle. "Pardon our intrusion, but might Claudia ask you something rather personal?"

"Of course, what troubles you?" Orla asks, leaning forward with interest.

"Do you perceive others' thoughts when you make physical contact?" Claudia whispers, her pale cheeks blooming with a rosy flush that spreads to the tips of her ears.

"Perhaps we should escort this assemblage to our homestead," Dave interrupts, clearing his throat. "We have several spare rooms. Not sufficient for everyone, but certainly preferable to camping outside."

"We'd be eternally grateful," Marie responds, casting a concerned sideways glance at Claudia's distressed expression. "A proper rest would benefit us tremendously after our... unusual journey."

*****

Dave, and now Orla's house is abuzz with frantic activity. Cormac and I gather musty wool blankets and down pillows from the cedar chest as the unexpected visitors, at least a dozen or so of them, will need to double up in each spare bedroom.

She pulls me aside into the shadowy hallway, her fingers digging into my forearm. "Do you feel it?" she whispers, her eyes wide with alarm.

"What? How they speak in that lilting, antiquated way? As if those ruffled collars and high-waisted gowns aren't costumes but their everyday attire?"

"But their souls," Cormac exclaims, her voice dropping to a hush. "They're vibrating at a different frequency, not dead but also not from this world or something."

A frigid draft slithers past us, sending prickling tingles up my neck like icy fingers.

"Thank you," a tall, willowy woman says as she approaches us, her long skirts rustling against the floorboards. "It's very thoughtful of you to give us shelter on such short notice. I'm Elizabeth."

As she extends her slender hand, a violent breeze rolls through the hallway; the lace curtains billowing away from the wall like ghostly apparitions. The floral wallpaper before me dissolves into mist, and suddenly, I'm immersed in a scene from centuries before, a candlelit parlor with a crackling fire and the scent of burning tallow.

"Molly, Molly!" Cormac urges, her warm hands cupping my clammy cheeks.

I blink rapidly, disoriented. Elizabeth has vanished. "Where'd she go?" I ask, my voice trembling.

"She went to fetch you water, worried by how pale you became. Is everything okay?"

"It's happening again," I manage to say through chattering teeth, my heart thundering against my ribs. "Just like three years ago."

"No!" Cormac's fingers intertwine with mine, her grip desperate. "We need to tell Orla and Dave immediately."

We rush outside through the wraparound porch and to the garden where they're gathering firewood, the air heavy with the scent of impending rain.

"What's wrong?" Orla asks, dropping an armful of logs as I double over, struggling to catch my ragged breath.

"Remember when I heard that voice three years ago? The one no one else could hear?"

"Yes, what did it say?" She snaps her fingers in the air between us, her brow furrowed in concentration. Then she jabs her index finger toward the sky, and says, "Drogen, no..."

"Drogheda," Alex says, his voice clear and confident as he and Claudia emerge from the house to join our circle.

"That's it!" I reply, a chill running down my spine at how he knew.

"There's so much we need to discuss," Claudia says, her eyes darting meaningfully to each of us, but she's interrupted by a woman with hunched shoulders and nervous hands who approaches on silent feet, tapping Claudia on the shoulder.

"Claudia, your mother's called a meeting," the woman says in a voice barely above a whisper, her gaze fixed on the ground.

"This is Lina," Claudia introduces her friend, holding a reassuring hand above the woman's thin shoulder. "Let's talk later." She waves, her silver pendant catching the afternoon light as they leave.

"And we need to get ready for work." Cormac's face twists into a grimace of disgust, her upper lip raising.

"Fine," I say, pushing out my bottom lip in an exaggerated pout. Then I turn to Orla, whose eyes are as big as saucers. "You sure you guys are okay with this crew crashing?"

"Of course," Dave says, his weathered hands gesturing expansively. "Already recruited a few guys to help fish."

"And others will help me at the dock." Orla's smile crinkles the corners of her eyes before she leans in to press her lips against Dave's salt-roughened cheek.

With that, Cormac and I step away further into the cool air. "Did you recognize anyone in the group?" she asks, her voice low and urgent.

"I don't think so," I say, searching through the foggy corridors of memory.

"That day by the lighthouse three years ago," Cormac says, her eyes distant as if seeing through time. "I know I was a bit out of it, but I swear there was a ship and some of those women were on it."

On the evening of January 25, 1921, Claudia Walker (r.)–the daughter of the late Mr. Sebastian Walker and his widow, Marie Edwards Walker–went missing along with three friends and the rest of the passengers and crew aboard the S.S. Hewitt. A search team is being organized, and the family is paying for travel. If you are interested in volunteering, please meet tomorrow, Friday the twenty-ninth at 9 a.m., at The Crestwood Shops located at 55th and Crestwood.

–FROM THE CLASSIFIEDS PAGE OF THE *KANSAS CITY TIMES*, THURS-DAY, JANUARY 28, 1921

CHAPTER TWO—ORLA
"We learn from failure, not from success!"
Abraham (Bram) Stoker

Dave and I slip through the weathered oak front door, the hinges protesting with a soft creak. Hushed voices drift like smoke down the shadowy hallway from the living room. After removing our shoes, we tiptoe across the worn floorboards, our socks muffling each careful step. His body, all that lean muscle, moves with impossible silence, a contradiction that leaves me in awe.

"I don't feel comfortable listening in," Dave whispers, his breath warm against my ear, eyes wide with apprehension.

"Spying is never my first choice," I say, tugging nervously at my sleeve. "But with Molly hearing that disembodied voice like three years ago and the sudden arrival of so many mysterious people, information is vital."

"It's not really spying though, right?" Dave crosses his arms tightly across his broad chest; shoulders hunched. "More like eavesdropping."

I press my index finger against my lips and then point toward the golden sliver of light spilling from the entryway further down the hall where the meeting is taking place.

"The Samhain Festival would be perfect for a wedding," Olinda offers, her melodic voice carrying clearly through the air.

I'm grateful we've shifted to a spot with a visual vantage point. Through the antique gilt-edged mirror across the narrow hallway, I can see Olinda's glossy black hair cascading past her shoulders and her obsidian eyes catching the amber glow from the Tiffany lamp. While I've met everyone at this gathering—the sincere man with the red silk tie, the woman with the umber shawl—I don't think I'd recognize each distinct voice in this murmuring chorus of strangers yet.

"I'll help with dresses and makeup," Florian volunteers, gesturing enthusiastically with ringed fingers.

"My fortune-telling is sure to be a hit," Nelly says, her bangles jingling as she adjusts her flowing scarf.

"Is that legal in this time and place?" Anna asks, one eyebrow arched skeptically. Though they don't share physical features, the identical head-tilt and questioning expressions of both Anna and Elizabeth are mind-blowing.

"Though we appreciate your enthusiasm in planning our nuptials," Alex interrupts, drumming his fingers against his knee, "shouldn't we be figuring out how to get everyone home?"

Dave's elbow nudges mine, his eyes meeting me with silent agreement. These people sound so lost; their voices tinged with an undercurrent of desperation beneath the wedding chatter.

"Mind if we join?" I ask, walking through the entry as Dave and I step onto the threshold of the living room.

"Of course," Claudia responds, smoothing her skirt. "It's your house."

"Did I hear something about getting back home?" I ask, scanning the circle of faces illuminated by the warm glow of table lamps.

Alex, the lanky man with blond hair, hacks violently, his Adam's apple lurching like something desperate to escape his throat.

"Yes, after the festival, of course," Marie interjects, her delicate hands fluttering like nervous birds. "We'll need to get back home."

"Half of us are from Ireland," Claudia adds, her triquetra pendant catching the light. Several people within the group raise their hands, Étaín and Róis among them. Étaín has hair that falls in waves like midnight water, deep brown with hints of auburn, while Róis's smile transforms her entire face, crinkling the corners of her eyes and revealing a small, endearing gap between her front teeth that somehow makes strangers feel they've known her for years.

"Oh, wow!" Dave slides into the empty chair beside Alex, the leather of the seat creaking under his weight. He leans forward, brow raised. "I hear the fishing's phenomenal there—pollack with that silvery sheen, wrasse flashing coral stripes, and flatfish barely stirring in the shallows." A few heads bob in agreement.

"And that it's beautiful," I say, imagining the sun striking glassy waves that shatter light into a thousand diamond fragments, jagged cliffs rising from the shoreline like the spine of some ancient sleeping beast, and emerald hills that undulate toward the horizon, their velvet slopes dotted with wildflowers that nod in the salt-laden breeze.

Elizabeth's fingers drum the tabletop. "Oh, it is just that. Which is why we'll need to secure passage back after the festival."

"Passage, like on a ship?" I ask, tilting my head. "Wouldn't flying be faster?"

Florian's cheeks pale; she presses a hand to her midsection and shifts in her seat as if the suggestion churned her stomach.

I clear my throat and change tack. "You can give us tips for Samhain," I say. "Since it originated in Ireland."

While they debate ancient harvest rites and magnificent bonfire superstitions, my gaze drifts to the ruffled curtains at the window. If they're not used to flight—Elizabeth talking about ships, Florian turning green—I wonder if they're even from this era. Anna's whispered question about fortune-telling's legality resurfaces in my mind.

I decide to press gently. "And where are the rest of you from?" My voice sounds too eager, even to me.

Florian straightens, forcing a smile. "Oh, we're from Kansas City, Paris of the Plains, reachable by automobile." She taps her fingers together, eyes darting.

Air shifts around me. Cars do exist now, but still—plane would be quicker. I bite back the correction. "Oh, so you're Chiefs fans!" I exclaim, making it casual.

"Chiefs?" Kiersten blinks. The word drifts over her like a strange echo. Dave's eyes meet mine, pupils widening.

Before I can untangle the moment, Dave stands and claps his hands softly. "We'll let you get back to your meeting," he says, voice smooth as oil. "I've got enough food in the fridge to feed everyone today, but for tomorrow I'll need to shift some from the deep freeze."

Kiersten is already at his elbow. "I can help," she offers. "We can chip in for our keep."

I exhale, catching Marie's eye. She's edging forward, lips curved in an inviting smile. "What can we do to help prepare the food?" she asks, voice warm, diverting attention.

A handful of the group drift toward the garage freezer, white frost crackling on the door. The rest follow me to the basement steps, where stacked bins of extra plates and tarnished silverware await. Each footstep echoes on the concrete, dust motes dancing in the single bare bulb's glow.

By the time we reconvene in the kitchen—pots simmering on the stove, the scent of chopped onions and garlic thick in the air—Ben and Kyle burst through the back door. Their mouths hang open; they freeze in the doorway. Ben, who had endured captivity alongside Cormac during that terrible incident three years back, runs the Ethel maritime museum, while his husband Kyle manages the local pub.

"You have visitors too?" Kyle's voice trembles, eyes wide as the freezer door.

"Yes," I answer, my tone hesitant. "But what do you mean by 'too'?"

Dave steps forward, guiding Ben, Kyle, and me aside into the narrow hallway. "Did you receive new arrivals at the pub?"

Ben rubs his palms together. "Yes. A group, about nineteen or twenty years old, and another group…" He frowns, jaw working as he hunts for words. "…who appear to be from the future."

The hallway falls silent, shadows stretching along the walls as if the very air holds its breath.

I squint at Kyle. "What exactly makes you think they're from the future?"

Kyle's eyes widen as he pulls a sleek, foldable rectangle from his pocket. "Their phones project 3D images that float in the air! Look what they gave me!"

Ben tugs on Dave's sleeve so hard I hear a thread pop. "And two of them look identical, down to the birthmarks. When I asked if they were twins, one laughed and said, 'No, I'm her clone.'"

I spread my hands. "So, your visitors have impossible technology, while ours speak in archaic English, and fainted at the sight of electric lights."

The floorboards creak. My voice must have carried more than I realized if Claudia heard me. She appears in the hallway entrance, Marie's shadow behind her.

"Clone?" Claudia's voice barely reaches us. "Vienna and Sierra?"

Ben and Kyle whip around so fast I hear neck bones crack. Their mouths hang open like broken hinges.

Claudia's lips curl into a knowing smile. "Thought so."

Marie steps forward, her face grave. "The reincarnated timelines have converged here, then."

My brain feels like it's filling with cotton. "The what?"

Marie squeezes my arm—I must make a face when visions of Ireland infiltrate my mind because she releases immediately, her touch warm through my sleeve before it's gone. "We need to return to our proper places before…"

The front door bangs open. A small boy stumbles in, face streaked with dirt and dried tears, eyes darting wildly around the room. Boomer, my border collie, and

Nessa, Dave's tan labrador, appear from nowhere, flanking him protectively, their tails low and serious.

I crouch down. "Hey there. Are you thirsty? Hungry? Lost?"

"Famished," he whispers, his voice small and sweet as a bell.

A gasp from the hallway. Elizabeth stands frozen, a single tear sliding down her cheek.

The boy's eyes lock onto her. "Mamma!"

26

CHAPTER THREE—MOLLY

"As you ramble through life, whatever be
your goal;
keep your eye upon the doughnut, and not
upon the hole." Irish Saying

We thought we'd left the crush of bodies behind at Orla and Dave's, but stepping into the tavern feels like plunging into another swarm. Pendant light glints off wooden beams overhead, and amber ale froths in kegs behind the bar. Cormac's band roars through a fiery solo atop the stage, luring half the fresh arrivals to sway in the aisles while I sling pints to the rest. Half of them are a motley crew—impermeable clothing protecting them, curious polished cubes humming softly in their palms—and their questions tumble over one another like loose coins.

I turn away, offering a sliver of privacy as two newcomers, Marrit and Sierra, step into the glow of a corner candle. Marrit's fingers, slender and sure, tilt Sierra's chin until her face catches the light; her fingertips hover there a moment before Sierra's lips rise to meet her. Marrit answers with a fervor that radiates warmth across the wooden floorboards. I feel blood rush to my cheeks at the sight of such unabashed tenderness. They pull back, smiling as if sharing a secret the world has never heard.

A vision overwhelms me like laughter from drunken lips. It's futuristic and includes a few of the newcomers at the pub. Before me I see Al working to save Vienna by creating a clone to take her place in a dangerous maneuver. Sierra's DNA was ripped from Vienna and replicated in a lab, her entire existence a manufactured duplicate, while Marrit was born thousands of feet above the ground in a metropolis that defies gravity itself, suspended in the clouds like a mirage! The vision flashing from a facility to a floating city is dizzying. As I shake my head, the vision dispels.

"You'll need to update Dave and Orla on these new arrivals," I say to Kyle as I peek my head into his office. I'm also drying the outside of a tankard on my apron, my hand moving in a circular motion that's become second nature.

"Are they opening an inn or something?" Ben chimes in, draping himself over the desk chair like a silk scarf tossed carelessly over a mannequin, one leg dangling toward the floor, his fingers drumming a private rhythm against the tarnished wood of the desk.

"Trust me, they'll have a plan and all the details soon enough," I reply, tucking a stray lock of hair behind my ear, feeling the cool metal of my earring brush against my fingertip as I do.

Kyle's gaze darts to the door, his eyes lingering on the tarnished brass knob, and the thin strip of light visible beneath the warped bottom edge. "You're okay to close up?"

"I am," I assure him, "and I think they can stay at the house." I nod toward Cormac's band still thrumming onstage. "Cormac's lease isn't up. We can crash there to-night."

Ben snorts. "Might want to carry your valuables with you, then."

Once Ben and Kyle vanish through the crowd, I slip around to the foot of the stage. A woman with a cascade of golden ringlets sashays before Cormac, as though enchanted by every note. My pulse hammers a warning—jealousy, sharp as a blade, twists in my chest.

When the last chord fades into the exposed ceiling like dissipating smoke, I guide Cormac's beautiful frame offstage back toward Kyle's office with its peeling paint and perpetual scent of coffee grounds. My mind flashes to the last time we'd been in that room with Oliver, his bloodshot eyes darting between us, fingers drumming an anxious rhythm on his thigh as he leaned forward, desperate for answers we couldn't give him. The hallway's low light casts long shadows on the rough walls. Inside the office, the battered desk and two stiff chairs sit under a single pendant light's glow. Cormac leans against the desk, her posture regally relaxed despite the evening's chaos. Her eyes glow like sunlit amber, and where the lantern light kisses her cheek, I catch the soft dimple that appears every time she smiles at me.

"We've raked in plenty in tips tonight," she says, voice warm and unhurried. "You good?"

I run a hand through my red hair, feeling the ache in my shoulders. "It's a lot of fuss for so many people."

Cormac's fingertips press gently to my arm, and her lips quirk in that crooked grin I adore. "You don't usually balk at rowdy crowds."

I huff softly. "I do when they hover the stage." I study the gloom beyond the door, willing my fluttering heart to steady.

She taps her chin theatrically. "I am a talented singer, after all. Admiration comes with the territory." Her tone is as soft as foam settling on a pint but as unbending as steel. I surrender with a sigh.

"Sorry," I murmur. "I'm nervous because I need to ask a favor."

Her hands settle on my shoulders. "And?"

"I thought we'd stay at the apartment," I say, keeping my voice casual. "Offer the house to the newcomers."

"What about my art?" Her brow arches, half in challenge, half in jest.

I open my mouth, then close it. She laughs, a gentle melody. "Just kidding. I can pack it."

"Probably wise," I say, and her breath fans my neck as she drifts close, lips tracing my skin at the nape. A shiver ripples through me.

"Shall we share the good news?" I murmur, voice husky with desire.

"Yes, but first..." Cormac's eyes pin me, fierce and tender, and without hesitation, she presses her mouth to mine.

*****

A slender woman with sharp, inquisitive eyes steps forward to speak for the group. The man next to her has eyelashes so long they cast spidery shadows across his cheekbones when he blinks, dark and feathery like the tips of calligraphy brushes dipped in ink. "I'm Austria, and this is my husband, Josh." They look almost too young for marriage, but their smiles hold a steady confidence. She ushers her curly-haired best friend, Tiffany, into the circle—the same blonde who danced before Cormac so entranced.

"We have a place for you to stay," I announce, Cormac's arm brushing mine in support.

"My crew usually finds lodging," Josh says, stretching his shoulders. "But a warm bed is always welcome."

Cormac grins. "We might be short on beds, but at least it'll be cozy."

A woman with daring eyes and ink swirling across her arms steps forward. "That works. I'm Ceresa." She offers a firm handshake. "I just so happened to have our packs when we…" she cuts herself short.

"Molly." I clasp her hand. "We'll need name tags for you all."

The newcomers beam. Tiffany steps up, hope blooming on her face. "What can we do to help close?"

Just then a man—Luke, by the sound of his easy greeting—loops an arm around Tiffany and pecks her cheek. "That band was incredible."

"It felt like home," Tiffany says, and I realize my own jealousy was misplaced.

"If you could wipe tables and stack chairs, we'd be most grateful."

"Absolutely," Tiffany says. "I run a restaurant back home; a few of us do."

"I can help too," Luke offers, already gathering rags.

Cormac exchanges a glance with me. "Perhaps when Samhain hits, you and friends could lend a hand again."

With extra pairs of hands, closing Shabby Tabby is a breeze. The night air is crisp as we walk the group the few blocks to our house—no single vehicle could have held them all. Packs bundled over shoulders; they chat and laugh under a sky freckled with stars, organizing themselves into turns for rooms and the lower floors.

Vienna, Sierra's DNA source, wrinkles her nose as a rusted blue sedan rattles past, leaving a cloud of gray-black fumes in its wake. "What is that acrid smell?" she asks, her voice tinged with disgust.

"Exhaust," Cormac says, but when Vienna's perfectly arched eyebrows knit together in confusion, she elaborates. "From the car." She points at the ruby-red taillights disappearing around the corner.

"Oh, does no one drive a poli-magno here?" Vienna steps off the cracked concrete sidewalk, the heel of her pristine black boot tapping experimentally against the rough asphalt. Before she can venture further into the street, her love Al gently wraps bionic fingers around her wrist and tugs her back to safety.

"What's a poli-magno?" Cormac asks.

"A poli-magno uses magnets to polar project from magnetic painted streets in order to move."

"I would love to see that happen but, no, our cement streets do not have magnetic paint, nor do our cars have magnets like that."

"So, your cars predominantly run on gasoline?" Vienna asks.

"We do have electric cars, but yeah, that electricity mostly is acquired by burning fossil fuels!"

Approaching the house, I'm still proud of the two-story Victorian with its arched doorway of carved oak and shuttered windows framed by climbing rose bushes now showing signs of preparing for dormancy. The slate-blue paint Orla had insisted on still gleams in the streetlight, catching light like the sea on a clear day. We'd planted those rosebushes together, arguing over the placement of each one, and now the earthy fragrance of the developing rose hips welcomes me home. I run my fingers along the wrought-iron gate that Orla had restored herself, hoping the house that had witnessed our laughter and tears would now embrace Cormac and me for the years to come.

Once inside, I slip away to pack essentials with Cormac's help. In our shared room, she gestures toward some of the newcomers as they inspect our remote controls since they differ so much from their strange devices and glowing cylinders. I stuff treasured trinkets and documents into a bag, then look up as Cormac gathers her canvases.

She pauses, eyes flicking over me, and my cheeks warm. A sudden, wild urge to claim her—fingers tangling in golden strands; mouth crushing hers—rises fierce in my belly. I swallow it down, focusing on the bags at my feet.

Once everyone's settled, we make our way to the apartment. I hook her artwork onto the empty walls. One painting, a mysterious portrait of me half-shrouded in shadow, catches my breath. "Is that…really how you see me?"

Cormac drapes her chin on my shoulder. "Half enigma, half open book—a room of mirrors and hidden doors."

"Shall we practice again?" I ask, voice low. "With so many newcomers, we might need to…well, decimate a target."

Her hands press to my hips. "Not when surrounded by my art," she teases.

"Fair enough." I lean in, lips brushing hers.

Cormac draws me near, and I catch the subtle break in her breathing—that telltale pause that sends heat rising to my cheeks and sparks a yearning deep within me. She wraps her arms around my neck, and our mouths collide in urgent, desperate kisses. The graze of Cormac's teeth against my collar sends electricity down my spine, delicate yet deliberate, like the first whisper of autumn wind through summer leaves. When her hand finds its way between my thighs, cupping firmly against denim, my body responds without thought—lifting, seeking, desperate to dissolve the fabric barrier between us. Her jacket falls to the floor before her fingers unbuckle my belt. Every nerve sings; the heat between us blazes.

A shrill ring shatters the silence like glass breaking inside my skull. My heart doesn't just sink; it crashes through my ribcage into a void. Cold sweat erupts across my skin as I wrench away from Cormac, her face blurring as panic floods my vision. My fingers, suddenly numb and clumsy, scrabble desperately for the phone. Orla's name blazes on the screen, a warning flare in the darkness. She never calls this late. Never. Unless it's dire.

"Molly, there's been a body found at Bethel's Landing."

I clutch the phone like a lifeline. "No…not again!"

CHAPTER FOUR—ORLA
"Keep love in your heart. A life without it
is like a sunless garden when the flowers
are all dead." Oscar Wilde

Though the scene before me rips my heart
to shreds, I'm strangely relieved that Molly
has Cormac in her arms this time. The
memory of her frantic pacing in our
cramped living room has haunted my night-
mares for three years, each echo of her footsteps a blade twisting in my gut. Last time,
a body was found just after Cormac vanished, leaving Molly to fear it might be her.

"Absolutely not," Marie snarl whispers,
her voice slicing through the cold air.
"Have you forgotten the misery that spell
unleashed? The insatiable need for reincarnation?"

I'm glad that we're in a secluded section of Bethel's Landing. Normally, police
wouldn't allow civilians near crime scenes,
but in our small town, they've realized it's
inevitable. They set up safe areas nearby

for us instead, and the rest of the town is in a different section than us. The body is close to the water's edge, mirroring the scene from three years ago.

"But without that, I'd never have met Alex, the love of my life!" Claudia retorts, arms crossed like armor.

Marie's exhale is a storm cloud. Elizabeth adds, her tone icy, "I'm with your mother on this." I'm grateful that Elizabeth left her boy at the house. This is no place for a kid to be.

"Tell me more about this reincarnation," I say, voice barely more than a tremor. They share a brief, loaded glance before Claudia jerks her head toward the corpse across the way surrounded by tall grass and shells.

Oliver lies there—once Dave's rival at sea, then our fierce protector. His body, marred with old burns, is unnervingly still. I remember the guttural howl that burst from him when the demon claimed him, how, in that leather-bound journal's pages, we found the rites to shatter the curse. Some of his flesh fell away as the wraith fled, and we thought him saved—yet here he is, dead.

A white-hot fury surges in me, only to be drowned by grief so raw it nearly crushes my ribs. A single tear carves a path down my cheek. Dave's hand, warm and reassuring, brushes my arm. Our soul-possession practice has become completely natural; our spirits entwine, and now he grants me the power to slip into any living soul without a touch.

"What can this spell actually do?" I demand of Claudia in a hushed but firm voice.

Elizabeth's hissed answer is a thunderclap: "It can snatch someone back from death, but the cost would hollow you out."

"How?"

"Because it's more like resurrection instead of reincarnation, and it causes ill-effects like the illness that took my life at the very beginning of all of this."

My heart hammers against my sternum. Beside me, Cormac kneels as close to Oliver's side as she can get. "It's the same spirit as before," she murmurs, voice rough with emotion, "but this time it's anchored, stronger."

Marie's gaze darkens. "We have to discuss this, now."

Molly presses against Dave's side, voice breaking. "I used to hate him. I never thought I'd feel this… void."

Her tears fall onto Dave's sleeve, a silent testament to loss. The coroner's zipper snaps shut, final and merciless. A hush descends as the newcomers form a tight ring around us.

"Let's move to the pub," I say to Molly, trying to steady my voice as more townsfolk have arrived, spilling into the section we occupy. "We can't be discussing magic here."

Molly pulls out her phone, thumbs flying. "Let me check with Kyle," she whispers, already summoning us to our own private council.

*****

Luckily, Kyle's fine with everyone meeting there after close. Even the unexpected newcomers show up, far more than just those bunking with Dave and me. I clear my throat. "Thank you all for coming. One of us is dead, and we're in more danger than we realized."

Cormac's voice is low and grim. "Agreed. This…presence that seemed to arrive with you won't vanish without a brutal fight."

Molly's jaw snaps shut on a curse; she snakes an arm around Cormac's shoulders like a shield.

Dave's eyes glitter. "First, let's take stock of our weapons."

"Weapons?" Alex echoes, brow arching.

I turn to Claudia. "Right. Two things: you wanted to know about hearing thoughts through touch, and you mentioned casting some spell."

Claudia swallows. "Ever since…time traveling, I can tune into people's minds."

"Wait, time travel?" I sputter. "Before that, how did you even know to ask me that?"

Marie's voice drips foreboding. "You're going to want to sit." Alex yanks a chair, and I sink into its embrace.

They spill everything about Cromwell's dark force stalking them across fractured timelines.

Marie gestures, nodding toward Elizabeth. "When my sister fell ill during the Siege of Drogheda, I—or rather, who I was then—reincarnated her." Her finger shifts to Claudia. "I did the same for myself and for Barnabus, my husband in that life. The gift passed to our daughter." Her voice drops to a whisper. "Even Cromwell himself, the man behind the siege, demanded reincarnation. He couldn't bear to be parted from Elizabeth; he loved her too much to let death separate them."

"Due to an incident that occurred in the future of the reincarnated souls, Cromwell sent counters, people created through magic, to fight us," Alex says. "Unfortunately, the soul of his reincarnated love, Anna, paid the price, and we traveled back in time to try to stop Cromwell at the beginning of all this."

Austria's eyes darken. "Our timeline diverged when Cromwell's soul returned. He sought control of the portal realm, and we fought him—myself, Josh, and the others who became like family to me." Josh's arm slides around her shoulders, a gesture both protective and reassuring. She draws a steadying breath. "It was during this timeline that Cromwell created the counter world you call home."

I shiver as goosebumps prick my skin: reincarnation shuttled their souls through endless worlds, but victory only spawned a shadow realm, ours. Counter world. Every syllable tastes like ice in my veins.

"In the future, interplanetary travel is common, and Cromwell abducted my dad, so I traveled to rescue him but found more sinister things occurring," Vienna says. "To save the world, I underwent an experimental medical procedure. Clones, war, and love—I finally beat Cromwell by sending telepathic messages that caused him to have a heart attack; hence, the counters sent to the past as well as this counter world were born."

They each awakened to their past lives at different moments, and Claudia's soul is entwined with mine. That's how she sensed my soul-possession gift. Her memories have been unclear since arriving in Ethel, so she wasn't completely sure.

"Alex, can you amplify her power, like Dave boosts mine?" I ask.

Alex's eyebrows hitch. "How would I do that?"

to ask about that later when there's more privacy.

Sierra folds her arms over her chest, the material of her impermeable jacket creaking, and Marrit's jaw tenses, a muscle twitching visibly beneath his cheek.

A sleek, midnight-black crow with iridescent feathers suddenly swoops down from the ancient oak beams of the exposed ceiling, its wings beating the stale pub air into miniature whirlwinds as it cuts past our huddled group and through the weathered door with its peeling paint. I don't remember the door being cracked open; its rusty hinges allowing a sliver of light to slice across the worn floorboards. When I return my eyes to the group, I notice Elizabeth's clutching Marie's slender forearm, their wide eyes tracking the bird's path with an intensity that suggests this is no ordinary crow lost in the dim, smoke-hazed interior of Shabby Tabby.

Sierra, her midnight hair catching the light from the dusty windows, cranes her neck and rises on tiptoes, leaning around the circle of tense bodies to scan every shadowed corner. "Has anyone seen Yesha?" she asks, her voice carrying a tremor.

"Yesha is my fiercely loyal best friend," Vienna says. "She's the one with blonde hair and an athletic build…she even guided me through the shimmering, nauseating portal between worlds for my first interplanetary journey," she trails on but stops herself.

I look around. "No, I haven't seen her."

As quickly as the interruption began, it ends when Austria steps forward, her tall frame casting a long shadow across the circular table with its constellation of drink rings and carved initials. How strange—something feels off, like the subtle wrongness of a familiar room where all the furniture has been shifted an inch to the left, a creeping sense of doom crawling up my spine like shivers. There's no time to focus on that foreboding or allow my spirits to plummet into the pit forming in my stomach.

"We're able to travel to a counter-like world and back to ours," Austria offers, twisting a strand of her hair nervously. "Could we do that here?"

"How?" Alex asks, eyes widening with interest. "Do you travel back and forth like stepping through a doorway?"

"No!" Josh stops Austria from answering, his hand shooting out to grasp her wrist. "Your trips are limited…wait, are you stuck here now?" He looks at Austria, his face pale with concern, a bead of sweat trickling down his temple.

"Our nemesis held a different name, not Cromwell," she says, gently pulling away from his grip. "So, I think we start from scratch here, in this land."

"No one's traveling yet, but it would be good to know the mechanics in case it does come to that," Alex brings the point back home, tapping his fingers rhythmically against the metal canteen at his hip.

"It's mostly psychological," Austria responds, her gaze distant as if seeing through dimensions. "The first time I traveled by accident when I had an adrenaline rush—heart pounding, vision tunneling. We should practice with everyone like we did with our team."

"So long as it's only practice," Josh's eyebrows raise as he responds, the skin across his left brow stretching taut.

Fatigue finally drapes over us, heavy and satisfied. We didn't even check on Oliver's crew—tomorrow, maybe. Dave and I step out of the pub together; sudden fog surges around us, tendrils like skeletal fingers. One coils around my leg, squeezing with cold malice. I stagger, wind knocked out. Dave's arms catch me, anchor me, and hold me. All the way home, even while driving, he clutches my hand until our safe return.

Inside, desire seizes us like magnets snapping together. Our soul-possession hums beneath our skin, demanding connection. His hand slides to my hip, the other barks at the nape of my neck, and his lips hunt down my ear, brushing heat across the soft swell of my throat. My head tilts back, offering more, and his kiss deepens, insistent, devouring.

By the time we crawl to the bedroom, clothes are discarded like shed skins. Fingers map every curve; a guttural moan tears free of me as he coaxes my body to arch, pressing harder, faster. Pleasure coils through me, hot and electric, as his mouth follows a trail of heat down my collarbone. I glide my hands over him, tasting him, every nerve alight, relishing his breath catching. We shudder together, bolts of raw ecstasy fracturing through us, our need a blazing supernova. I've never needed anything more.

CHAPTER FIVE—MOLLY

"It's my rule never to lose my temper till it would be detrimental to keep it." Seán O'Casey

After a blissful night with Cormac following the horrible finding and enlightening discussion at the pub, we're preparing candles for Samhain with the crew crashing at our house. As Vienna cleanses candles with incense, she opens up about some trauma she and her friends went through in their timeline. It's still difficult wrapping my brain around the fact that they're from the future where interplanetary travel is a common occurrence, not only for the super wealthy.

"How did you survive all of that—medical experiments, physical abuse, and imprisonment?" I ask Vienna.

"I have good friends who helped me." They gather for a group hug—her clone Sierra, best friend Yesha, all of them.

"When she wasn't trying to save the day herself," Al adds with a smirk. Then he kisses her on the forehead.

Yesha's eyes narrow as she leans forward. "And without getting revenge," she says, her voice dropping to a whisper that somehow fills the room. She notices a glossy black feather clinging to her sleeve, delicate as a secret. With pursed lips, she exhales a precise stream of air that sends the feather spiraling toward the floor, where it lands without a sound.

"You guys had to deal with medical experiments?" Austria asks. "So did we. Did yours center around organs?"

"Did you have conscience and memory transplantation in your timeline as well?" Vienna asks.

Austria's eyes go wide in shocked terror. "No! Ours were more for the purpose of gaining the ability to transport through a portal to another world."

"You didn't have Fifth Dimension Friction Inhibitors to travel astronomical units?" Vienna asks.

"I don't even know what that is," Austria responds, exasperated. "Is that how he transported us here?"

"Not just you guys," I say, "but the group staying with Orla and Dave too."

"No, it wasn't that," Al says. "It was like nothing I've ever experienced. There was a static sound, things spun in a vortex around us, and the ground dipped away."

"I think you need to talk to the other group," I add. "They seem to know a lot about reincarnation and time travel."

"Why don't we call them?" Cormac asks.

So, I call Orla. After a bit of confusion from the other group, apparently talking over speakerphone on a call is new to them; the groups discuss their travel here. Claudia, having a deaf ear, is closest to the phone. It's a wee bit overwhelming, talking over each other until it's finally Vienna and Austria doing the talking.

"Your trip here sounds a lot like ours—time travel, but I noticed something different with it in this instance." Claudia takes a deep breath before continuing. "This time a cold dread coiled in my gut because something evil underpinned the passage."

Both groups go silent with that. Then a breeze rolls through the room, but only my hair is swept to the side by it. Everything around me fades away, and I'm immersed into a scene from centuries before.

Old rickety wagons roll across a dirt street, but what catches my attention most is a woman I recognize as Elizabeth from the other group. Instead of being bound in rope as Cormac had been in my vision three years ago, she lies on the ground—blood dripping down her chin.

"Molly!" Cormac's in front of my face, waving her hands. "You went away for a moment there."

"What did you see?" Vienna's eyes bore into mine as she asks the question.

I tell them what I saw and how it's different from before, including how my visions precluded Cormac, Ben, and our Oliver almost dying three years ago. When I mention Elizabeth being part of the vision, the group on the phone speaks up.

"It's most definitely him!" Elizabeth says.

"No," Marie interjects. "He brought two souls into one and ended his reincarnation cycle in the seventeenth century! He cannot actually be present here. It must just be remnants of his magic."

"And yet his spirit is here," says a voice that's both a happy thought and anxiety inducing. Gordan's ancient and powerful presence permeates the room. The broody-looking Gorta is ironically named Gordan. Gortas surfaced during the horrific Irish famine. They look starved, but their power gives them the ability to feed entire populations. They don't just feed on forms of food but also spiritually. He's always had such a knack of reading situations early, which must be how he knows about the spirit who's barely made its presence known now?

"How do you know that?" I ask him.

He turns his skinny, tall body toward me and smiles. "As someone with the power to feed large groups of people spiritually, I can sense when a presence is draining them."

His words deplete me, punching right into my chest. Will this ghost be able to take control of a body like last time, or is this to be more like psychological warfare?

"Is he trying to repeat the Drogheda Siege again?" I ask.

"Wait, that no longer happened," Claudia says loudly over the speakerphone. "We traveled back in time and stopped it or at least stopped it from being successful."

"You, what?" I gasp. "No, I remember it clearly."

"That's because this is his counter world," Gordan says.

"What does that mean?" Cormac almost yells, putting her hand on her chest. "I'm real! She's real." Then, she puts her other hand on my chest to show how real we are.

"You're real indeed, but you were transported here," Gordan says. "You all need to get back home, it seems."

"But this is all I remember," I exclaim.

"Think harder," Gordan answers as if it's that easy. "And his spirit isn't going to let any of you travel as long as he's capable of controlling that."

"Orla?" I say into the phone. "Do you think you and Dave could tap into a spirit's thoughts?"

"You're asking this of us again?"

"I'm sorry your ability is so awesome."

"Awesome it is," Gordan adds.

Claudia's voice can be heard in the background, but I can't make out what she says.

"Claudia wants to help," Orla informs me.

"I must meet Claudia." Gordan's eyebrows raise.

"Yeah, she has possession abilities like Orla, and her partner, Alex, has abilities like mine," I inform him. "Since we lost Oliver, we've been trying to accumulate weapons to fight this spirit."

"Quite intriguing!" Gordan taps his chin in contemplation.

"Um," Cormac says. "Can Claudia and Alex bring their best friends with them when they come over here?"

Gordan and I both turn to Cormac with perplexed faces.

"It's just," she starts, "while I've been trying to get a read on our ghost, a couple thoughts filtered in…since both soulmates have powers, it might be a friend instead who complements their half-blood abilities."

Gordan nods, completely in sync with these thoughts. I ponder for a bit and decide it's not bad to have the numbers. I don't want to lose anyone else.

*****

Once they arrive, we're giving lessons under the ancient oak tree in the backyard; its gnarled branches casting dappled shadows across our makeshift training ground. Orla, her skin gleaming in the sunlight, demonstrates with Dave how they first complemented each other through possession. Dave's eyes glaze over slightly as he pushes forward specific memories—his childhood dog, a sunset over the water—navigating Orla's soul possession instead of letting her wander unchecked through the labyrinth of his mind. Their fingers intertwine as they progress to him visualizing a certain person, becoming a living bridge for Orla's abilities.

Next, Cormac and I explain our connection, how her slender hands become my conduit, channeling energy like electricity through copper wire. Alex's face softens when I describe the telltale ringing, like a teakettle whistle, that precedes death. Relief floods his eyes as he realizes he's not alone with this burden. Further out in the clearing, we push aside fallen leaves with our boots. Cormac's melodic chanting rises and falls like waves as I face the wooden target. When I open my mouth, the sound that emerges isn't human, a banshee wail that vibrates through my teeth and splits the air. The target doesn't just break; it explodes into splinters that rain down like deadly confetti.

"Wow!" Alex says, aghast. "I can do that?"

"Once we find who complements you."

Sierra's gaze drifts away from the target that has captured everyone else's attention, finding instead the weathered oak fence at the property's edge. There, Yesha balances with arms outstretched; her impermeable boots carefully testing each step along the narrow, splintered rail. The wind blows through her blonde hair as she wobbles slightly, regains her footing, then continues her precarious journey with the focused determination of an Olympic gymnast on the balance beam.

"What was that chant?" Josh asks Cormac as he and Austria approach us.

Before she can respond, the foghorn from the lighthouse blares loud enough for us to hear it all the way here. It's not the normal issue that would emit IF the lighthouse were operational but an incessant long toot. The wind picks up, rattling neighboring chain-link fences and wind chimes to no end.

Next, a booming, low voice rumbles through the yard. "You can't stop me now," Cromwell's spirit barks through the air. "I'm more free than I've ever been. A body is so overrated. Now I have no bounds!"

I clench my hands into tight fists; my nails digging half-moons into my palms as rage burns through me like wildfire. There's no mistaking it—his spirit haunts this place, a palpable presence that shivers through the air, far more substantial than mere lingering traces of his magic.

Elizabeth's son tilts his small face toward the vast expanse of sky, his eyes searching the gathering air between wisps of clouds. "Father?" he calls, his voice thin and hopeful against the breeze. Seconds stretch into a hollow silence; the space remains mute, offering neither comfort nor recognition to the boy's plaintive question.

Black wings beat against the air as a crow launches itself from the oak fence, leaving behind a single obsidian feather that spirals to the ground. Drifting higher on a thermal current, its beady eyes lock onto a rust-colored hawk circling above. The crow approaches with deliberate stealth, razor-sharp talons extended like miniature daggers. In one fell swoop, the smaller bird becomes a missile of fury, colliding with the surprised hawk and plunging its pointed beak deep into the raptor's exposed throat. A shrill, guttural cry pierces the countryside silence before the

entangled birds plummet in a chaotic tumble of feathers and blood toward the hardened earth below.

CHAPTER SIX—ORLA
"To learn one must be humble. But life is
the great teacher."
James Joyce

"Wasn't it the journal you found that held
the key last time?" I call out to Dave, my
heart hammering as the echo of that disembodied voice still thrums in my skull.

He snaps his fingers, the sound sharp in
the hush of the room we ran to after Cromwell made himself known. "You're right."

"Where is it?" My words come out
strangled, desperation seeping in. Memories rush back: seeing a drifting shadow in
the lantern room of the silent lighthouse,
Oliver's crew trembling at night to voices
only they could hear, and the way Dave and
Molly vanished into that hidden chamber
while Cormac and I held a séance over ancient tombstones. That's where we un-
earthed the journal: in the dusty, cramped
alcove behind a secret door at the end of my
hallway. A cold prickle climbs up my arms.

"We found it in the weird room behind the concealed door at the end of the hall in this house," Dave says, rubbing his forehead as though the recollection aches him.

"You okay?" I whisper.

"Yeah, yeah." He clears his throat. "That was something else. It felt like the house reached out and yanked Molly and me upstairs. We clung to banisters and doorframes, but the pull was too strong. Then an invisible force wrapped us together with rope." He shudders, every syllable tremoring.

"Would you mind describing what the journal looks like?" Marie asks.

"But I was the one who realized that house was the epicenter of every oddity back then," Gordan interrupts, his voice low and measured. "And that the key to confronting Cromwell lay within that diary."

"That's right," I say, fingers brushing the edge of the table. "Could you bind wards around us again?"

Gordan's brow furrows. "I haven't pinpointed the central locus yet. My wards can shield only one structure; otherwise, I'd seal the entire town."

I pace the floorboards. "Back then, the lavender and rope combo banished Cromwell."

Marie's voice cuts through the air like a blade. "That's MY JOURNAL you're talking about!" Her eyes flash with sudden fire.

My heart hammers against my ribs. "How the hell did your journal end up here?"

She leans forward; her knuckles white against the table's edge. "When you've been entangled with a monster like Cromwell as long as I have," she hisses through clenched teeth, "nothing sacred stays safe. He's taken so much, why not this too?"

I delicately lean toward her. "Then maybe you'll have the answers we need. If we replicate that ritual now, do you think it'll banish this 'counter-world' since he did the whole two souls in one body thing?"

"I believe so," Marie murmurs, her tone now soft as a lullaby. "Because once we do, we all go home."

"Yeah, if we even know what that is," Molly grumbles, arms folded.

We exchange glances, those of us from Ethel, wondering what home feels like now. Will we remain a group, or fracture once the veil falls?

"So, the whole town just…shifts to another realm?" I ask, turning to Marie.

"I do believe so," she replies, tilting her head in thought. "Your true memories should snap back once you leave this place."

Molly squeezes Cormac's hand. "Will we forget everything that happened here?"

Dave crosses his arms, and I picture the family portraits that line our staircase in the old house, generations of Ethel faces staring down.

Cormac glances up. "What if we enlist help from stronger spirits?"

"That's an excellent thought," Gordan says, eyes brightening.

Cormac moves to clear the cluttered table. "How many extra settings do we need?"

"Three," Gordan answers without hesitation.

"A Silent Supper," I say as realization blooms. "Everyone eats in silence to reach across the veil. Which spirits should we call?"

"And what are their favorite foods?" Molly adds, as though reading my mind.

"What should we meditate on to guide them in?" I prompt.

We fall silent, each turning over names in our minds.

"Our Oliver," Molly finally says, her eyes filling with tears. "He was possessed by Cromwell—he might know the enemy's weaknesses."

"I've been inside his head," Vienna offers, voice calm.

"You what?" I gape.

"In my time, I communicated telepathically." She shrugs. "I also dispatched Cromwell, showed him visions of his own cruelties until his heart gave out. Doing that put me in his mind."

Gordan's mouth forms a small O of awe.

We pile the table with seafood: plump scallops for Oliver, crispy crab cakes for Jenny—our old roommate who Cromwell once resurrected in that macabre display—plus buttery shrimp for one of Gordan's lost magical friends. Makeshift crates serve as chairs for some of us, wobbling under our weight.

The supper begins. Candles flicker, silverware clinks, and at first only the sounds of hungry mouths fill the space. But as bellies fill, a thick silence seeps in: legs bounce, fingers twist, eyes flick from face to face. A chill winds down my spine, as if ice water trickles across my bones.

I think of Oliver's haunted gaze, of Jenny's laughter snatched away by the bonfire that devoured our senses. I brace for her voice on the wind—but instead, a rough, husky bark shatters the hush. Chairs scrape; forks clatter on plates.

I glance at Gordan. That voice isn't Oliver's, not even in Cromwell's grip.

Marie and Claudia exchange quick whispers, their faces grave. Claudia has to turn away from us as to place her hearing ear toward Marie.

"What is it?" I demand. "Do you recognize him?"

"Unfortunately, yes." Claudia sighs.

Marie's lips curl. "What a skid rogue!"

Their circle turns toward her, eyebrows raised.

"Not only did Cromwell forge a counter-world," Alex says, regret coating his words, "he also created a couple counter souls as I mentioned before. The voice was one of them."

My stomach plummets.

"Wait, weren't those spirits becoming enemies of Cromwell?" Claudia asks Marie. "Maybe they'll side with us."

"As if we can trust them!" Marie snaps.

"Let's at least hear them out," Gordan advises, calm as ever.

"Ruarc, Aodhán, are you there?" Marie calls into the dusky air.

A rasp answers, grating and slow, "What…is…this…place?" Ruarc's voice, Marie mouths to us.

"Do you remember the siege you attempted?" Marie prompts.

"We asked to be freed," Aodhán's response crackles through. "This isn't freedom!"

"Cromwell interrupted my spell to free you," Marie reminds them.

"Or you trapped us here!" Ruarc snarls.

"If I'd meant to imprison you, why reach out now?" Marie argues, frustration flaring.

"What do you want?" Aodhán demands.

Before Marie can reply, I blurt, "Are you two alone?"

Marie's finger shoots to her lips, but it's too late.

"Who's that?" Ruarc's voice trembles.

"My friends are here," Marie says. "And you won't believe who's haunting us."

"No!" Aodhán's bark echoes. "Cromwell's dead!"

"Um," Cormac says gently, "so are you."

Their absence is immediate. The rancor in the air vanishes; Ruarc and Aodhán are gone, offering no guidance. We never contacted Oliver, Jenny, or Gordan's friend; we're adrift. And now there could be three adversaries instead of one.

Gordan exhales. "Three robes armed with crossbows, their shadows have haunted us all along."

I press a trembling hand to my mouth. His words bring back the surreal nightmare in Dave's barn I had three years ago. What in the actual fuck!

Liam, one of Alex's friends from Ireland, leans forward, his face illuminated by the dining room pendant light that casts long shadows across his hollow cheeks. "Claudia, are you able to cast the Ulster curse on spirits?" The dark circles beneath his eyes seem to deepen as he fixes his gaze on her. His lips part into a wolfish grin, revealing naturally straight teeth. "It would be perfect if you could knock them out while we devise a plan against them."

Gordan's weathered hands grip the edge of the oak table. "You know the Ulster curse?" His voice drops to a whisper. "What else do you know?"

"You better not be asking only her," Étaín snaps, tossing her hair over one shoulder. Her brilliant lopsided smile graces us as she straightens her spine. "Many of us from Drogheda know magic."

The air lightens with eagerness as Étaín's coven describes binding spells that can paralyze an enemy mid-stride, while Elizabeth's friends whisper of healing balms that can mend shattered bones and purge poison. Gordan's pen scratches frantically across paper, recording every word. Marie's fingers twist nervously at her collar as she mentions her leather-bound journal; its pages yellowed with age and stained with herbs, hidden somewhere around here. Despite this arsenal of supernatural weapons at our disposal, cold apprehension pools in my stomach. How will any of this work in a realm crafted by our enemy? The nightmare of those three men with their evil eyes and stretched smiles haunts me still, lurking at the edges of my consciousness like wolves in the mist.

82

CHAPTER SEVEN—MOLLY

"Come little children, I'll take thee away, into a land of Enchantment. Come little children, the time's come to play, here in my garden of magic." Sarah Sanderson, *Hocus Pocus*

The next morning, pale dawn light glints off dew-damp fenders as Cormac and I, flanked by a few still bunked at our house, roll toward Orla and Dave's farmhouse. The air tastes of wet grass and promise. Our mission lay clear between us: discover whose gifts best amplify Claudia's and Alex's today. With Samhain nearing, we don't have a minute to lose. No sooner had we crossed the worn threshold into their wide, sunlit kitchen then Vienna's voice draws us into a tight ring. Everyone freezes, as though invisible cords pull us inward. "This time let's keep Cromwell out of our beeswax," she murmurs, her gaze sweeping each face.

My chest tightens at Vienna's words, her subtle warning hanging heavy in the air. I glance around the sunlit kitchen, taking in the tense expressions of my companions. The memory of Cromwell's intrusion into our affairs still lingers with them too, like a bitter aftertaste, leaving a cold knot in my stomach.

As the group huddles closer, I can feel the weight of the decision ahead pressing down on us. The task of uncovering whose gifts would best serve Claudia and Alex feels like a daunting challenge, especially with Cromwell's lingering presence. But there is no room for hesitation; we had a duty to fulfill, a purpose to serve.

Taking a deep breath, I square my shoulders and meet Vienna's gaze with a determined look. Despite the unease that settles within me, I know that we must work together for the greater good. With a silent nod to Vienna, I steel myself for the task ahead, ready.

"Gordan, can you raise that ward again?" Orla asks, her voice calm as morning mist.

He inclines his head, trailing long fingers northward toward the picket fence outside, then east to the old barn, south over the flowerbeds, and west toward the house itself, an invisible barrier shimmering only to him. I feel the hairs on my arms prick at the protective hum.

Unease slithers through me, recalling how Dave and I once discussed powers—and wound up yanked by a transparent force into that hidden chamber. We'd walked away convinced that even idle chatter could be bait. Clearing my throat, I say, "Dave and I thought talking powers last time was what lured us into that trap."

Claudia's brow creases. "Should we cloak ourselves, then? Or I could try the old Ulster curse."

Gordan lifts a skeptical eyebrow. "You doubt my warding? Besides, a crackle of that curse might tip them off if it even takes hold."

Claudia shakes her head, relief flickering across Gordan's angular features. Before he can speak, Florian bursts in, hair flying, eyes bright with excitement. Hands clasped as if holding treasure, she chirps, "I have the perfect cover!"

We all blink at her. "And that is…?" Gordan prompts.

"Wedding planning!" she cries, spinning once on her heel.

I stiffen. Wedding planning? My pulse bathes in equal parts intrigue and dread. Cormac flashes me a knowing look. How does she always zero in on my soft spots? I steal a glance at Orla, who merely shrugs, lips curved in mischief.

Kiersten catches Florian's elbow, grinning. "Efficiency aside, I do adore a good shindig."

Florian beams. "We'll pretend to scout Claudia's maid of honor and Alex's best man!"

I burst out, "Hold on, aren't we gearing up for a fight so no one else dies?"

Olinda's soft exhale drifts over us like a sighing wind. "Unfortunately unavoidable, considering Claudia's…condition."

The word "condition" strikes like frost. Orla's airway bobs; I bristle. "We don't shun pregnant women these days."

Leaning in close, Kiersten whispers of a parallel Ireland where centuries-old alliances with France and Spain had fast-tracked women's rights—a world where a rounded belly drew support, instead of invoking the need to control the mother's actions. I swallow a pang of envy for that reality; one I'll never know so long as we remain in the counter world.

Alex slides forward, brushing a gentle kiss across Claudia's hand. Warmth blooms in my chest even as apprehension coils beneath. Cormac's fingers curl around mine, her eyes shining with reassurance. I feel the fragile safety of us all, yet fear surges. I edge aside with Orla while most of our group goes out the door to the yard, voice low enough only for her. "I'm terrified for Claudia's fetus; its soul hasn't fully crossed over. Are we risking it? Is it closer to the ghosts that haunt us?"

Orla's brows knit. "We should get Gordan's counsel."

We return to reconvene with the small circle that stayed inside. As we share our thoughts, Gordan's face darkens in concern, then brightens like the sunrise outside. "We need to leave gifts for the fae, secure their favor."

Before I can scoff, Elizabeth's clear voice cuts in: "I'd like to help by gathering stones and crystals." She nods respectfully at Gordan. "In my faerie-touched past, the Tuatha Dé Danann were part of every hearth and clearing."

His expression softens almost to wonder. My own skepticism ebbs at the certainty in her tone. "Tell us what to do," I say.

Anna, Elizabeth's reincarnated soul, one birth removed, offers the nearby beach; I point to the wooded hills. Gordan adds the old quarry. Within moments, we've sketched a map of offerings in ink and paper atop Orla's table.

A cheer rises outside as Lina, Claudia's timid friend, shoots a triumphant fist into the air; Alex squeezes Thomas's hand in solidarity. Matches decided in moments; they pivot to training. Relieved shock overwhelms me. That was much easier than I'd imagined, almost too easy. It took Orla and me years to find someone who complemented our powers.

I catch Claudia's voice as Orla and I step outside, her words carrying a hint of unease. "It is rather strange hearing thoughts in your voice, like an echo chamber in my skull, especially on top of my tinnitus. It's usually so difficult to overhear anything!"

"You get used to it after a while," Orla says with a dismissive wave of her fingers.

"Helps differentiate your thoughts from others when they're wrapped in familiar tones."

As I approach Alex, I grip Alex's shoulder to steady him and remind him to focus only on his target when channeling his power. The memory flashes vivid in my mind: Cormac's face contorting with alarm, her eyes widening to perfect circles when I'd glanced at her mid-chant during my first power initiation. Her voice had risen to a panicked pitch as she'd practically lunged at me, fingers digging into my arm. "Don't you dare look anywhere but at your target! You want to blow up the wrong thing and kill us all?"

I tingle with anticipation, itching to hunt the stones that might sway the fae. Whispering to Cormac, I ask her to text me if the others need my assistance.

Soon, Ben and Kyle appear through the tall grass. Ben leads Orla toward the water's edge, the shore gilded by slanting sunbeams. Kyle falls in step with me as we plunge into the forest's orange hush. My heart gallops between purpose and fear. We kneel on mossy earth, filling leather pouches with smooth, vein-marbled stones and iridescent crystals, each chill bright in my palm.

Then the woods shiver, and a heavy dread ripples through me. A sudden gust snarls through branches; the shadowed canopy overhead thrashing like an angry sea. An emptiness yawns around us, wrapping us in a cold embrace. I hear footsteps crunching in the undergrowth, but when I stare between the trees, nothing moves. My heart lurches. Kyle's eyes widen beside me; he heard it too.

The footsteps become louder, and Kyle grabs my wrist. Then they are louder, approaching us quickly. We turn and sprint out of the woods, our breaths rapid. Fear takes over, and we sprint like never before. When we're out of the woods, I no longer hear the footsteps. Kyle lets out a breath of relief, wiping sweat away from his forehead.

"We'll sort this," I whisper, though my voice wavers.

"I'm worried about Ben," he replies, dread shadowing his tone.

"We have enough," I insist, trying to bolster both of us.

Unsteady legs carry us away from the murky depths and back to Orla's yard, lungs burning but pride alight.

Yesha's curious eyes find our collection, lingering for just a moment before she winces, throwing up her small hand to block out the metallic gleam that bounces off the jagged edges. Sierra pulls Yesha away, taking her back to where they'd been. My heart races as I check over my shoulder to make sure the others haven't looked our way. Gordan and Elizabeth volunteer to place the gifts under moonlight; they know the rituals best and fear fae mischief. I sink against the fencepost as Cormac pads over, settling a warm hand on my shoulder. Relief ripples through me, tangled with longing, but my pulse still rattles like wind-tossed twigs.

Claudia's voice slices through the clearing. "You're worried about our offspring and didn't think to consult us?" Her eyes flash with fury as she advances toward me, leaves crunching beneath her pumps.

Claudia's anger startles Alex, whose power veers wildly off course. It strikes an ancient oak with a sickening thud, severing the trunk. The massive tree crashes down, sending birds scattering into the pale sky, missing Thomas by mere inches.

"Sorry," Lina whispers, her slender frame seeming to shrink as she lowers her head, hair falling across her face. "She asked me to."

I straighten my spine, feeling heat rise to my cheeks. "I did not give you permission to linger in my thoughts," I retort, my fingers instinctively tightening into a fist.

"You lot were being so secretive," Claudia says, throwing her hands up. She exhales sharply, her breath visible in the cool air. "What did you expect?"

"We figured out a way to protect your offspring," I yell back, my voice echoing against the distance. "You're welcome!"

After a huff from Claudia, they all return to their practice. By the time they finish their drills and set off for our house, dusk has woven shadows between the fields. Cormac shepherds the stragglers home; I wander behind, my mind churning with worry for that embryo. At last, we slip through our front door into the hush of the apartment living room, walls humming with quiet.

"That was an intense day," she murmurs, stepping close. My chest tightens. I ache for her comfort yet fear my quivering nerves will spoil the moment. A soft laugh escapes me as I give her arm a playful jab, though my fingers tremble.

She brushes hair from my face, her eyes probing mine. This isn't just echoes of trauma; it is the living shadow of what we are now facing. I don't need words. I tilt my head, draw her in, and our lips meet—urgent and fierce. I taste her fear mingled with desire, as hungry for reassurance as for passion.

Her hands trace my ribs, dip lower, until the tight knot in my chest slowly unravels. She lifts me effortlessly, every heated breath a pulse against my neck. Garments slip away like old burdens, and her lips map every vulnerable plane. I brace for collapse but instead feel iron resolve forge in my chest. In this incandescent moment, her love is the strongest ward of all.

The Shabby
Tabby'
THE INCANTATIONS
Shabby Tabby
I.D Required
The Shabby Tabby

CHAPTER EIGHT—ORLA

"The new white yacht with tall slender masts restlessly awaited her departure. Above the din of bustle and confusion rose high pitched and excited voices. Groups of people stood on the dock and stared, while others were tangled in last minute embraces."

Cruise of the Northern Light, Borden

"I missed you the past couple of days," calls one of my regulars, his voice curling around the wooden pilings. Across the marina, Dave is crouched by a tangle of fishing rods and lines. His plaid shirt clings to the strong ridges of his back and arms as he untangles hooks and swivels, a living map of sinew and motion. The late-afternoon sun glazes each wave in molten chocolate, as though someone's dripped warm syrup across the rippling surface. A crisp autumn breeze threads itself through my hair, bracing and sharp, while I bend to harvest cockles from the sand, each shell glinting pale pink against the gray-brown mud.

Dave motions to Conor and Liam, demonstrating how to snap the safety latches on the downrigger and test the motor's remote kill switch. His hands move with practiced precision, fingers brushing over metal and line. Nearby, I show Neasa and Étaín how to sort and pack the cockles into mesh sacks for market: how to gauge the perfect size, how to rinse them after they've boiled. The two newcomers from Ireland learn faster than I expected, their nimble fingers organizing shells with uncanny ease. For the most part, their teamwork is seamless—though Étaín's barbed wit and quick sarcasm draw sideways glances from a few customers, who can't resist smiling at her boldness.

"Don't say it!" Neasa warns Étaín.

"Ah, sure, it's only a joke."

"Fine!"

"I'd help you, but I'm too shellfish." Étaín laughs while opening and closing a cockle shell.

A long shadow crescents across the water as a familiar vessel drifts into view. It's the weathered ship Oliver once captained; its timbers dark and swollen from salt spray. When it grinds to a halt against the dock, a dozen crewmembers file down the gangplank. They move with a sense of weariness that hangs heavy in the air; their expressions etched with a mixture of sorrow and relief. I lift my chin, straining to catch their conversation. Their voices carry the same rough edge I remember, rougher still now that their leader is gone.

"That's it," one man says, his tone as brittle as driftwood. "No more night runs for me."

"You and me both," another growls. "Oliver's dead and the voices are back. I'm done."

My pulse spikes. I meet Dave's eyes, and he drops the rod in his hand, legs flexing as he ducks under crates and leaps over coils of rope as if they were mere ripples on the dock. He's at my side in a heartbeat, chest heaving, concern and protective fire burning behind his dark eyes.

"What's wrong?" He pants, voice low, urgent.

I lean in, barely a breath from his ear. "It's Oliver's crew. They're hearing the voices again."

He presses his warm palms to my arms, his thumbs brushing reassuring circles into my jacket. With one swift motion, he flips my sandwich board from OPEN to CLOSED. It squeaks in protest, and a handful of customers grumble as he shoos them away. "We need to talk to the others."

In minutes, the newcomers are saddling into the borrowed truck. Liam—miraculously a competent driver after our grueling lessons—has loaded Conor, Neasa, and Étaín into the backseat. Dave's crew is already hitching lines and tying down gear while I slip my hands into his as he and I climb into his battered pickup.

He slides the door open and guides me into the passenger seat, his fingers settling warm and firm around my wrist. I remember a time, not so long ago, when he couldn't touch me like this. When I craved the safety of his arms but feared the invisible barrier between us—my soul possession shield, his adamant respect to honor my wish for distance.

The memory flickers bright as the day we finally made contact. I'd glimpsed his vision of our first kiss before I'd even known I wanted it. The shock of seeing his unspoken desire, his vulnerability, had stolen the breath from my lungs. Then, pressed together by fate and by fire, we'd learned to share, to trust. He'd complemented my power, helped me channel my touch without anger. That breakthrough had felt like sunlight bursting through storm clouds.

Now, with the truck's engine rumbled to life, I lean my head against the cold window, watching the familiar roads of Ethel blur by. The town seems to hold its breath, every lamppost, every shadowed storefront poised on the brink of some unseen gloom. As the sun sinks, the cold tightens its grip.

When we pull up to the old farmhouse, everyone is already gathered in the dim glow of external lights. Molly stands by the porch railing, her arms folded. Gordan paces the yard, muttering under his breath.

"They're really hearing voices again?" Molly's voice is tight, hopeful.

"Voices…plural?" Gordan presses.

"I'm certain they said 'voices,'" I reply, stepping out into the chill early night air.

Gordan's eyes narrow. "Last I saw, there were three figures in long robes, each shouldered with a crossbow."

Marie clutches her shawl. "What do you mean?"

I describe the vision—how the robed silhouettes had raised their crossbows in unison, how their chanting had skated down my spine like icy water, and how they vanished when Dave lunged at them in a desperate swing.

Elizabeth's small child hesitantly rounds the corner, straightening at the sound of our voices. "Mama?" he asks, eyes wide.

She kneels to gather him in her arms. "Yes, sweet one."

"Why are they talking about the nightmare I had last night?"

Every head whips around. Elizabeth presses her lips together, then gently slips her hand into the pouch at her waist. She offers him a handful of invisible dust, her "magic" to keep the bad dreams at bay. In our world of spirits and sight, perhaps it truly is magic.

When the child runs off to bed, Elizabeth's expression turns grave. She draws us close. "My son is cursed," she says, voice dropping to a whisper that crackles like embers in the air. "And we must break it."

Dave's brow furrows. "Why is he cursed?"

She tells us of her love for Cromwell, the ancient family curse that claimed their child. She had defied death itself to reincarnate the child, but that was before she broke the curse, so it still clings to him. The loss in the original timeline sparked Cromwell's grief, which had driven him to bloody vengeance time and again.

Claudia straightens her back. "How do we undo it? Can we get to Brú na Bóinne?"

I glance around. "What's Brú na Bóinne?"

Onóra, another traveler from Ireland with hair twisted into a loose braid, requests a map. Dave flicks open his silver laptop, its screen casting a blue glow across our faces as we huddle around the kitchen table. Soon we're tracing the jagged coastline around Drogheda with fingertips that leave smudges on the glass. I can't help but notice the similarities of Drogheda to Ethel.

I ask to pull up a map of Ethel beside the one we're currently looking at. The limestone lighthouse, the oldest building in town, glows faintly on the screen like a sentinel against the pixelated waves. Gordan, his voice dropping to a whisper, points out the rocky outcropping where the worst incident happened three years ago; his weathered index finger trembling slightly as it hovers over the spot. Its location in Ethel mirrors the location in Drogheda only closer.

"So, what's the ritual?" I ask.

Claudia raises an eyebrow. "Do we need horseshoes?"

"I have some in the barn," Dave volunteers.

Elizabeth unfolds the plan: we'll take something precious belonging to her son—something he won't notice is missing—along with iron horseshoes, up the lighthouse's worn stairwell. At the apex, we'll bind the curse with ancient words, call upon the spirits to banish it, then bury the relics in the earth around the tower.

"With Cromwell's spirit nearby," I murmur.

Gordan nods. "We'll need my warding."

"But it's his son," I point out. "He'll want to be involved."

"He would have supported breaking the curse," Elizabeth says softly, "but now…"

A plan sparks in my chest. "We do it during the battle, while he's distracted."

They all study me for a moment, then one by one, nod. It's a good plan, desperate but necessary.

That evening, as they go their separate ways to retire, my heart flutters between victory and fear. Dave draws me into his embrace, his warmth enveloping me like a promise kept through the years. In the amber glow of our room, my fingers trace the familiar landscape of his chest, rising and falling with breaths that have synchronized with mine through a thousand nights. He kisses my forehead with such tenderness it makes me ache, his eyes holding mine with a devotion that still steals my breath after all this time.

"We'll keep them safe," he promises.

"And they've got years of experience fighting Cromwell's fury," I add.

He arches an eyebrow. "We still haven't sifted through his thoughts."

I press my forehead to his. "No need to charge headfirst into more danger."

He laughs and lifts me effortlessly, carrying me toward the bed. "Trust me," he whispers against my skin.

His lips meet mine like a promise fulfilled, tender as moonlight on water. My fingers trace the contours of his face, memorizing every line as if sculpting a masterpiece meant to last forever. Time surrenders as he lays me down, whispering my name like a prayer against my skin. Each kiss along my collarbone feels like poetry written in a language only our bodies understand. My shirt falls away, forgotten, as his reverent gaze makes me feel both vulnerable and cherished. We move together in perfect harmony, two souls finding a home in each other's arms, creating a sanc-

tuary of love that even the approaching
tempest cannot breach.

CHAPTER NINE—MOLLY

"Sail forth—steer for the deep waters
only,
Reckless O soul, exploring, I with thee,
and thou with me,
For we are bound where mariner has not
yet dared to go,
And we will risk the ship, ourselves and
all."
Whitman

Flipping the heavy wooden picnic table on its side in the backyard demands every ounce of my strength. My palms sting against the rough-planked surface, and I feel the grain bite into my skin as I lever a corner upward. The late afternoon sun slants through branches overhead, sprinkling flickers of light across the grass and illuminating a fine haze of dust that rises with the table's movement. Once the tabletop settles flat against the earth, I plant my shoulder against its edge and shove, my leg muscles coiling and releasing in powerful thrusts until I hear the soft scrape of wood sliding across soil. My breath comes quick and warm, mingling with the sharp scent of crushed clover underfoot as I steer the table toward the spot I've chosen.

It is nestled in a hollow ringed by wisteria vines; their lavender blossoms cascading like delicate chandeliers in the half-light. We're spoiled in Ethel with magical blooming wisteria every year for Samhain. Tendrils of sweet, musky perfume drift around me as I pivot the table into position. The wood settles on uneven ground with a final small tilt, and I press the lantern—tall, slender; its metalwork etched with curling leaves—onto the center plank. The glass panes catch the fading daylight, turning pale blue like ice before the flame goes alight. In my pocket, the velvet ring box burns against my thigh, as though it knows the moment I've longed for is at hand.

From my other pocket, I retrieve my phone and thumb through the playlist I've curated, the soft crescendos and tender piano chords that will underscore what I plan to say. I step back, heart humming, and drink in the view: wildflower grass brushing the table's legs, the lantern's promise of warmth, the wisteria petals drifting in a lazy spin. This is the place I will ask Cormac to marry me…before Samhain, before her band embarks on tour again, before fate can snatch tomorrow away. The thought unsettles me: Ethel may not have a tomorrow. None of us knows where we'll end up or if we'll even stand together after the battle. My fingers close around the velvet box as if squeezing it might anchor me to courage.

Deep breath. Determination steels my steps as I turn and head back toward the house.

Inside, soft light pools around Dave's upright piano in the corner. Kiersten's voice lilts through the room: "I've always wanted to play. Usually, my days are filled with the grind, but here I actually have time." She perches on the piano bench next to Cormac, who leans in with a patient smile. "This white key to the left of the two black ones grouped together is a 'C'," Cormac explains, nudging Kiersten's thumb into place with gentle precision.

The piano's varnished wood looks warmer beneath their fingertips as I settle into a nearby chair, unwilling to break the tender bubble of instruction. Kiersten's eyes shine with concentration. Cormac guides her through "Twinkle, Twinkle, Little Star" in soft syllables—"Thumb twice, ring finger twice, then pinky"—and each note rings clear in the hushed room. When Kiersten masters the tune, Cormac gently unfolds a cluster of music sheets from her tote; their edges crisp and smelling faintly of ink and possibility. She shows Kiersten how the lines map to the piano's octaves, how the notes' shapes govern rhythm, and Kiersten lights up with understanding.

I stand and drift forward, heart swelling, then press a soft kiss to Cormac's cheek. She turns, surprise crinkling her eyes. "Creating another musical monster, are we?" I tease.

Cormac brushes loose hair from her forehead. "Better to provide entertainment. They're cooped up and scared out of their minds."

"Who's scared?" Kiersten pipes up, puffing out her chest. "I'm not afraid of anything."

We exchange amused glances. Kiersten blushes and admits, "Okay, maybe a little scared."

Cormac places a comforting hand on her shoulder. "We're going to figure this out and keep everyone safe."

From the front door comes Florian's cheerful summons: "Kiersten, can you help me carry these rolls of material inside?"

With renewed purpose, Kiersten leaps up and dashes away, leaving the soft echo of her retreating footsteps. I turn to Cormac, heart drumming. "Will you come outside with me for a moment?"

Her brows arch in playful suspicion. "So secretive." But she follows, sliding past the doorframe into the dusky air. My pulse is as rapid as a drumroll.

We step around the house and into the shadowed grove where lantern light flickers among wisteria blossoms. Cormac inhales sharply, eyes widening. "What's all this?"

I point to the table and the lantern's glow, then sweep a hand across the gathering dusk. "Please sit."

She lowers herself onto the bench, petals drifting into her lap. "What is it?"

Before worry can cloud her face, I drop to one knee, velvet box poised in my palm. Lantern light shimmers off the metal hinges.

"Molly!" she breathes my name.

"I'm incomplete without you," I say, voice unsteady but fierce with conviction.

She covers her mouth, eyes glistening. "And I'm incomplete without you," she begins, then pulls away. "But now's not a good time."

My chest tightens. "It's as good a time as any," I plead. "If not now, when?"

Her gaze drops. "We're facing so much, so many people depending on us."

"But that's precisely why," I insist, apprehension nibbling my bones. "We have to seize what we can while we can. There may not be another chance."

She looks away. "Give me a moment," she whispers, voice distant.

Panic flares. "Is there someone else?" I blurt, as if the question might shield me from rejection.

Her expression hardens. "You know there isn't." She stands abruptly. "I just asked for time, and you jump back to this. I thought we were beyond jealousy."

Her words sting as she storms back inside. My heart splinters. I've let my fear wreck everything.

*****

"This is your fourth," Kyle intones, voice low and insistent, shadows flickering in his eyes. "Maybe you should slow down."

"I'm fine," I grind out, jaw tight. "Everything's fine."

"Perhaps some food would help," he suggests, tone edged with warning.

"Why couldn't she have just said yes?" I snap, heart pounding.

Kyle shrugs. "A lot is unraveling around here, if you haven't noticed."

"I don't need your lectures or your food," I hiss.

"Whatever you say," he replies, glancing at Ben.

"I'm going to the docks," I declare, pushing back from the bar stool. "The sea breeze might clear my head."

"Don't you always complain about the stench of fish there?" Kyle asks, amusement dark at the corners of his mouth.

"At least let me drive you," Ben insists, catching my arm as I turn away.

"Fine." I release a breath I didn't know I'd been holding.

He offers advice as we walk to his car. "Give Cormac some time. You two are terrified of commitment, but you're meant for each other. Trust me."

I force a smile, tracing the outline of storefronts and the café window where Claire waves. Goosebumps crawl up my arms when we pass the lighthouse.

When we park, I spot Dave a few spaces over with Claudia, Alex, and Marie. Austria's sleek car follows, packed with Josh, Vienna, and Al. A covert meeting? Why wasn't I invited?

"Maybe now's a good time for you two to talk," Ben says, nodding toward Cormac. "And you really should've eaten."

"Thanks for the ride," I mumble, hurrying to the edge of the dock.

A blood-curdling scream shatters the tense quiet. My muscles lock. It's Cormac—her voice frayed with terror. Wind snarls around us, snatching at a spool of rope that's begun to unravel. One strand coils around Cormac's ankle, another around Orla's leg, yanking them off balance. They tumble, flailing for purchase as the rope tightens like a noose.

Dave and I exchange a frantic look, then sprint toward the water's edge. My lungs burn as I launch myself forward, but the rope drags them inexorably toward the sea. They grab at railings, rotting wood, anything to stop their slide into oblivion. Memories of invisible hands dragging us up that blasted stairwell flash across my mind, but this force is merciless.

They're carried up the gangplank of Oliver's ship—bound together by the rope's cruel weave. The plank jerks skyward before we can climb it. The vessel groans as it pulls away, taking them toward the yawning darkness of the open water. I want to scream, but the knot in my throat chokes the sound.

We leap into a waiting skiff. Dave's fingers dance over the ignition, and the motor coughs to life. He motions for me to drive, and then we charge after the retreating ship, salt spray stinging my face.

As we near Oliver's hull, Dave yells, "Hold her steady!" and swings onto the ladder. I grip the throttle, heart hammering, haunted by the wind's monstrous roar.

The ship's engine slows, and I adjust to match the change in speed. Dave's head appears over the rail. "I untied them, but they're shaky. I'll bring her in closer to shore—follow me."

We slip alongside and dock with rattling chains and creaking boards. I leap onto the deck, breath ragged. Cormac stands trembling, eyes wide with raw relief. I wrap her in my arms. Orla sinks to her knees, clutching a battered journal—its cover stained with salt and dread.

"Is that what I think it is?" I whisper.

Orla can only nod.

Dave kneels beside her. "We should take that to Marie. Maybe it holds the answers we need."

A voice slides through the gloom, low and mocking: "I wouldn't do that if I were you."

My blood runs cold. "Who's there?" I demand, scanning the shadows.

Dave frowns. Orla's lips tremble—she hears it too. The wind carries the final, venomous words: "Trust Marie," it says, and I recognize the whisper of our greatest tormentor…Cromwell.

CHAPTER TEN—ORLA

"I was born on the night of Samhain, when the barrier between the worlds is whisper-thin and when magic, old magic, sings its heady and sweet song to anyone who cares to hear it."
— Carolyn MacCullough, *Once a Witch*

Falling asleep after hearing that voice again is agony. The sheets feel stifling, my mind racing with echoes of his rasping tone, each syllable chilling my blood. I twist and turn, desperate for rest, until dawn's pale light seeps through the curtains. Yet morning brings clarity: today, Dave and I will delve into Cromwell's thoughts and seize the knowledge we need to stop him. As terrifying as my first spirit possession sounds, I fear more what that ghost might physically do to us; like the rope that had ensnared Cormac and me.

I lie in the soft glow of sunrise, reaching out for Dave's warmth only to brush cold emptiness on the sheet beside me. My fingers encounter something foreign: a cluster of oak leaves whose veins run like tiny rivers, a sleek security card etched with shifting holographic sigils, and a still-warm chocolate chip cookie; its dark morsels glistening under the light. Bewildered, I swing my legs over the bed and hurry to the window, where Dave's truck sits quiet in the drive. Heart pounding, I race downstairs.

The main hall buzzes with visitors clustering by the hearth, shoes scuffling on wood floors, and Boomer's thunderous barks as he lunges at Yesha. The scent of freshly brewed coffee and baking bread floats through the air. "Boomer, outside!" I call, weaving past startled guests.

"Have you seen Dave?" I ask Elizabeth.

"No, dear, but there's been so much activity that I easily might have missed him," offers Elizabeth, wiping her forehead with the sleeve of her dress.

A full sweep of the house doesn't get me anywhere, so I head outside to look there.

Worry sets in as more and more ground is covered, but there's no sign of Dave. Fear curls in my chest as I approach the barn. The door creaks open to stale straw and drifting dust motes. I sprint down the aisle of empty stalls, panic gnawing at my insides. Frustrated, I flee back inside, up to our room, where I left my phone on the bedside table. My foot taps as I call his number. The ring echoes once, twice, and then I hear it: a faint buzzing from his side of the bed. Cold dread spreads across my skin. Bolting downstairs, I almost miss a step.

"Has anyone seen Dave?" I shout, voice breaking. "I can't find him anywhere, and his phone's upstairs, and his truck's in the drive."

Claudia is the first to approach me, concern shadowing her face. Vienna is quickly behind her as well as Austria.

"When did you last see him?" Claudia asks.

"We went to bed together, but he wasn't there when I woke up," I pant.

"He hasn't been down here that I've seen," Austria adds.

"Did you notice anything out of place?" Vienna inquires.

I take a deep breath, recollecting. "It's really strange, but there were items on the bed in his spot."

"What items?" Claudia ascends a stair.

"Leaves, an advanced security card, and a chocolate chip cookie, of all things."

"Can we see them?" Vienna also ascends a stair. The women exchange a worried glance before we go upstairs.

Standing in our bedroom, the women look at the items, puzzling over their meaning.

"We used oak leaves like this for our time travel spell," Claudia speaks first, holding a leaf between her fingers.

"Dave doesn't know that spell," I murmur, shaking my head.

"How did a Planet Vortex facility card get here?" Vienna picks up the card to inspect it further, its surface rippling with light.

"And this looks just like one of my grandma's cookies in our portal world. She sprinkled sugar on top just like this."

"None of this makes sense!" I say, exasperated.

"Cromwell transported us here," Claudia says, face darkening. "Could he have transported Dave?"

"Can we ask the spirits if they know what's happened?" I plead.

"I don't see why not," Claudia responds. "I'll gather everyone."

I call Molly, voice trembling, and ask her to bring everyone else over, including Cormac and Gordan. She asks what's going on, and when I tell her that Dave has disappeared, that he's been taken, she gasps.

"We'll find him and get him back," Molly assures me. "I promise you."

Pacing in the living room, waiting for everyone to arrive, an idea surfaces. Our last contact with a spirit had not been very effective, and we don't have room for that now. If I could possess the spirit's soul, I could be guaranteed answers. Then I think about how Cormac had complemented another half-banshee before Molly. If she was able to complement more than one person, perhaps Lina can also complement my soul possession abilities in addition to Claudia's.

I'd ask Claudia to handle the soul possession, but I worry she's so new to it that something could go wrong. It would also be good to have the process be as stealthy as possible with the least amount of people involved.

"Lina," I whisper as soon as I'm next to her. "Will you come over here for a moment?"

"Sure?"

Once we're tucked away in the office, I begin immediately. "I need to ask a favor. I normally wouldn't, but it's a bit of an emergency."

"What is it?" she asks.

"I need you to complement my ability so that I can read the thoughts of the spirit."

"Uh, I don't know." She chews on her bottom lip.

"Maybe we could practice now on someone else," I suggest.

"On whom?"

"Molly," I say as soon as the thought arises. "She's my best friend, has knowledge of this, and will understand if she senses it."

Morning light slants across cluttered papers as Lina holds out her hand, and I grasp it. The usual tickle scurries its way up my arm. As the connection completes, I catch a glimpse of her sepia-toned house in 1920 Kansas City, floral wallpaper curling at the corners. I push forward the image of my old roommate, Jenny. I squeeze her hand to remind her to look for Molly. The vision moves as if we're walking. It doesn't have to go far before we see my front door through Molly's eyes.

"Orla!" I hear Molly yell from the front door.

"You're ready," I tell Lina as we release the link. "Be sure to sit by me when we commune with the spirit."

"Will it be Jenny, the woman you showed me?"

She would be the most helpful I believe. "Yes."

Approaching Molly and Cormac, I feel determined to find Dave. Before too long, Gordan has us all sitting at the dining room table with one extra seat and crispy crab cakes on the table in front of it.

"Should we consult my journal?" Marie asks.

Molly and I look at each other, remembering Cromwell's words: I wouldn't do that if I were you…trust Marie.

"If this doesn't work, that is the first thing we should do," I reply to Marie, and she nods, though I can see she's a bit upset.

Summoning Jenny's spirit is a mix of excitement to hear an old friend but urgent as well because it's vital to find the information we need.

"Molly?" Jenny's voice is bittersweet to hear. "Orla?"

"Jenny!" Molly speaks, knowing this is a charged moment. "How are you?"

"I'm connecting with other positive souls. How are you?"

"We need your help," Molly says, leaning forward.

Lina grasps my hand, and we're traipsing the world that Jenny currently resides. Everything's lit up with a soft glow. Bright light shines through foliage so colorful it looks as if it were painted. Further out, water sits at the edge of a cliff, looking like an infinity pool. Concentrating hard, I look beyond that and see dark, jagged mounds shrouded in fog.

"How can I help you?" Jenny asks Molly.

"Dave has disappeared, and we believe an evil ghost recently added to your realm is responsible."

"I try to stay away from negative souls, but I have noticed a rather loud new addition."

Lina and I view Jenny's memory of seeing Cromwell's spirit, like a storm cloud thundering, and it takes everything in me not to gasp in shock. He's among the jagged mounds and now I see fire breathing out of them. Beyond them everything looks abandoned apart from the mold and decay that keeps them company.

"That's understandable," Molly says. "Have you noticed any unusual activity?"

"Well, now that you say that, this soul does seem to have two shadows."

Two small clouds, I assume are the counters, come into view. We spoke to them the last time we communed with spirits. The top of the clouds seem to be in the shape of hats. Tendrils of the two clouds float from them as if hands stretch out to grab us.

"What about activity to reach our world by the negative spirit?"

Lina and I hear Cromwell chanting in her memory. He says, "I banish you left, I banish you right, to a different time, where you'll be out of sight." This is followed by the vision of a town from long ago, with cobblestone roads and lanterns swaying in the breeze. It fits the description some of the newcomers provided of their home, 17th century Ireland.

Apprehension twists my gut. If Cromwell has ripped Dave into another time, how will we ever bring him home?

"May the road rise up to meet you, may the wind be always at your back, may the sunshine warm upon your face…"
— An Irish Blessing

Cormac's brush moves in slow, deliberate strokes across the canvas that sits on an easel in the apartment's living room. Warm afternoon light filters through the gauzy curtains, dancing on the oils, and the gentle sway of her arm catches the sun in molten moves. With headphones clamped over her ears, she's created her own private sanctuary amid the clutter of unfinished sketches and paint-splattered rags. I swallow hard, every nerve taut with the memory of our recent catastrophe, and yet there is no time to unpack the disaster of that proposal. First, Orla and Cormac had been yanked, tethered by rope, onto Oliver's ghost-ridden ship. Then that same will-o'-the-wisp of a spirit had plucked Dave and flung him across dimensions into another era. Now I'm left scrambling for answers. My heart aches at the thought of heartbreak, but I refuse to let the same fate befall Orla, not if I can help it.

My messenger bag lies by the door, its leather seams straining against the weight of the key hidden inside. I snatch it up, shove my feet into laced-up boots whose rough leather smells of dust and damp, and march toward the door. I fling it open with a clang of metal on wood and holler, "I'm heading to Shabby Tabby to drink an entire bottle of Jameson!" The boards creak underfoot, but Cormac doesn't even glance in my direction—either she didn't hear me over the music, or she is deliberately ignoring my theatrics. I try again, more theatrically: "Going to light a bonfire in the courtyard!" Silence. So, I pull the door shut and set off through the chill of early evening, leaves crunching under my boots as I make for the café, where I hope my message has reached Marie.

The front of the café glows with warm lamplight, its chalkboard sign boasting today's specials in looping white script. I push open the door and am met by the hiss of the espresso machine and the smoky perfume of toasted pastries. Claire, behind the counter, spots me immediately. "The usual, Molly?" she asks, her tone gentle as steam rising from a new pot of coffee. I nod, muscles aching from tension. Claire turns to Marie, seated by the window in a slatted-wood seat. "And what will you have today?"

Marie looks up, her eyes alight. "Do you have any loose-leaf tea?" Claire blinks, surprised by the request. "Or a hot herbal infusion, anything you might steep yourself?" Marie adds, her voice as soft as petals. Claire smiles, retreating to rummage through jars of cinnamon and chamomile.

I slide into the seat opposite Marie, the old table's surface pitted and scratched, and ask, "Why loose leaf?" My tone is casual, but inside my heart thumps.

Marie closes her long coat around her and gives me a slow, knowing smile. "I may or may not have a knack for reading tea leaves." She tilts her mug, tracing imaginary runes on the porcelain surface.

I push the worn leather journal across the table. Its cover is cracked and mottled; the brass clasp dulled by years of handling. "I may or may not be in need of precisely that talent," I say. "But first, let's see what secrets these pages hold."

She reaches out, fingers brushing mine as she opens the journal to a ribbon-marked page.

Steam curls from our drinks as Marie's eyes dance across the inked lines. Three years ago, we'd used similar information to banish Cromwell's lingering presence, a haunting that had turned our nights into sleepless vigils. But this new spirit form feels different: malevolent, more insidious, like a creeping rot taking hold of our world from the inside out. I watch the way her brow furrows at passages describing memory-wiping spells and traveled dimensions.

"My recollections of past lives have always been crystalline," she murmurs, voice low. "But here…everything's fuzzy, like looking through mist."

I frown. "If traveling to this world blurred your past, might leaving it do the same to me?"

She fixes her gaze upon me. "Perhaps. But we could weave a protective charm, one that anchors essential memories and bonds with each other." Her offer warms me, and I nod.

"That would be splendid. But first, can we restore your own clarity? Those reincarnation recollections, if they come back whole, might guide us."

Marie begins to recount the story written in the faded entries: how, in 1649, Elizabeth died and left her coven shattered, how she and Oliver Cromwell had been consumed by grief, how Marie had, in desperation, reborn Elizabeth, and accidentally brought Barnabus along. Speaking his name makes her lips tremble; Barnabus is nowhere to be found in our Counter World. Cromwell himself had forced the bond, ensuring he, too, would be reborn—and in doing so, altered history. Their defeat flung them here, stranded among time-woven souls.

Then Marie's eyes gleam as she leaps ahead to the 1920s, to the Prohibition–era coven that had harnessed wild, musical magic in speakeasies behind velvet curtains. Mary, her original self, had guided the first circle, but like Barnabus, Mary is missing now. She worries that without those potent rituals, our power here is dulled. That's why our modern acquaintances, travelers who slipped between the Counter World and our own, are so vital. They bring forth knowledge of interdimensional travel, even if their journeys are limited. And beyond them, futuristic souls, pilots of superluminal speed and engineers of consciousness transfer, have technology that can reshape our struggle.

A spark lights in Marie's eyes. "Perhaps our victory lies in uniting every fragment of knowledge—past, present, future—as a single team rather than lone avengers."

I lean forward, the edge of my seat creaking. "Brilliant. But what's our first step?"

Marie closes the journal with a soft snap. "We restore those reincarnation memories, everyone's. Once each soul recalls its tapestry, the patterns of Cromwell's sabotage will become clear."

I exhale. "Do you know a spell that can do that?"

She taps her temple. "I believe so. The strongest conduit is Claudia. She never needed a spell, born into the cycle of rebirth itself."

I press her. "Which souls are Claudia tied to?"

Marie lists them: no seventeenth-century echoes in her bloodline as it's the original, but threads from Austria and Vienna. Then her gaze swings to me. "You, too, are reincarnated. Kiersten, Tiffany, and Yesha among your facets."

My breath catches. "Then what happens when this world and its mirror-counter world fade away? Will Tiffany and I become doppelgängers in the actual world of this time?"

Marie taps the table in thought. "Perhaps. Spiritual doubles rather than identical faces."

I shift uncomfortably. "All our energy's gone into Cromwell; what about Ethel and its people?"

"You're in peril in Ethel as long as he lives," Marie says quietly. "You remember what happened three years ago; Cormac was nearly lost."

I bristle. "That's a little manipulative."

She smiles, gentle but firm. "You're right. We can focus on more than one battle. Now, memories first."

Night has fallen by the time I lead Marie down the narrow lane to my ramshackle house. The streetlamps glow amber, and a few leaves cling to skeletal limbs. Inside, we find a handful of our mystical allies already assembled for Samhain: travelers with secrets in their eyes, ready to combine old coven rites with modern know-how. Austria and Yesha stand in the corner, their fists darting in practiced jabs through invisible opponents.

"Good," Austria coaches. "Control your adrenaline, then we refine projection. Once you master it, you'll vanish from here and reappear 'home.'"

I walk toward the main group, where Vienna's voice rises in haunting song: "And all still circled the pond that had pooled, in only heartbreak and sallows…" The words send a shiver down my spine.

"Those lyrics are my family's," Claudia says. "My mother sang them."

The circle forms around our dining table, and each woman lights a candle: Marie, Elizabeth, Olinda, Nelly, and Claudia. The table holds a glass of blue-tinted water that swirls like captured starlight, Nelly's shawl embroidered with moon phases, and a dagger whose obsidian handle gleams as though alive.

Their chant begins low and guttural, an echoing rhythm that makes the floorboards hum. Goosebumps chase across my arms. Elizabeth lifts the dagger, rotating it between delicate fingers as she speaks words of consecration. Nelly raises her shawl high, her voice proclaiming that this was indeed the time and place. Marie intones solemnly, "We stand upon the threshold of worlds." Olinda and Claudia, voices entwined, call for all that was lost to return.

At first, the air holds its breath—then a flicker of light, subtle as a star's first wink. A torrent of memories crash into me. I double over, clutching the table's edge as images flood my mind: a smoky speakeasy lit by chandeliers, Florian's tailored dress gleaming under red lanterns, Kiersten's gloved hands checking hidden pockets to avoid the rum smuggler's gaze. Then, a sudden shift: I am springing from behind a tombstone in a haunted house, squealing patrons recoiling in delight. Finally, I hover in a city floating on clouds, Sierra's silhouette aloft against a cerulean sky—until a great wing sweeps across the lens of my vision, cutting the scene away.

I straighten, pulse thrumming in my ears, breath ragged. Around the circle, flickering candlelight dances on faces alight with revelation. Marie nods to Claudia, and in a voice as clear as chimes, Claudia proclaims, "I elevate all power within this circle, collected from this spell, so mote it be." Their chant swells again, full of ancient force, and despite every tremor of fear inside me, I rise onto shaking feet and join the dance. The circle spins, our voices rising, and in this moment, I know we are truly united—across centuries, across worlds, together ready to beat back Cromwell's shadow once and for all.

Drogheda was known for its impenetrable defenses, but Cromwell had a plan. He brought in powerful siege artillery and relentlessly bombarded the town walls. After an ultimatum was rejected, troops stormed the town and slaughtered any resistance. Even civilians were not spared. This event is still considered an awful stain on Cromwell's reputation today. It took place on September 11, 1649.

CHAPTER TWELVE—ORLA

"May joy and peace surround you, contentment latch your door. And happiness be with you now and bless you evermore."
— An Irish Blessing

We move around the forest clearing where the Samhain Festival will unfold, lavender and cedar smoke spiraling in lazy, aromatic clouds. The air carries the sweet, resinous bite of cedar mingled with the floral softness of lavender, an energetic cleansing that seems to brush away every lingering worry. I wish we had a ritual for unwanted ghosts; surely they're no different from stubborn negative energy, but for now, this fragrant swirl will have to do. When the smoke dissipates, we kneel and scatter coarse grains of salt in a ring around the perimeter, each white mote catching the light like tiny stars. I'd love to extend this barrier to the lighthouse, but Marie's scribbled notes warn that Cromwell's presence must remain undisturbed in that territory.

A hollow ache pulses in my chest. I wish Dave were beside me. I miss his laughter, the reassuring weight of his hand in mine. At the center of the clearing, a great felled tree trunk—gnarled with age and flattened on top—serves as our makeshift altar. Draping it with black velvet is easier with two people's help, but I smooth out the folds alone, the fabric swallowing up bits of loose bark. Soon we'll invite guests to lay photos of their departed loved ones here. I place Jenny's portrait against the velvet, then Oliver's, each photograph a stark reminder of lives bright and gone.

Across the way, Nelly arranges her crystal ball atop a circular folding table she's brought in. Its glass surface gleams under a shaft of light as she cleanses it with a soft cloth, preparing for the first festival readings. Even her calm concentration draws a small smile from me. Near the trunk, Molly places the Death card from our tarot deck smack in the center, anchoring it with smooth river stones; charcoal-gray, heavy in the hand. Florian drifts through us with a basket of dried florals and amber leaves, weaving wreaths for visitors to hang over doorways. Later, as dusk deepens, townsfolk will light candles in their windows, guiding kindly spirits back home. We used to build a roaring bonfire to ward off harmful spirits, but after the catastrophe three years ago, we no longer do that.

Claudia sets a polished silver scrying bowl onto the velvet altar. The bowl's mirrored surface reflects the flickering light from between the trees in rippling patterns, perfectly suited to the temporal puzzle we're desperate to solve. Molly mentioned that the visitors seemed to have an aversion to discussing saving Ethel, and I'd asked Claudia previously about it. According to her, the worlds with counters, beings created by Cromwell through magic, had been troublesome. She had almost died due to one, so they had a fear of all things counter. She leans toward me, voice low. "I believe we can see Dave. Perhaps even speak with him. Would you like to try?"

My heart flutters, and the dull weight in my chest lifts for the first time. "Yes. Tell me what to do."

"In 1921, I used my soul-possession ability to witness past events, so long as the person I linked to was reincarnated from that era."

"That sounds a lot like my bond with Dave," I mutter.

"It is; except I observe externally, like peering through a window in time, rather than inhabiting a spirit." She closes her eyes. "Touch my arm. Focus on the moment you want to see."

Instead of arguing that indeed Dave's complementing my ability is entirely similar, he had shown me Oliver and a group of people preparing for the festival three years ago like an observation instead of thoughts; I press my fingertips to her forearm. A cool pulse tickles beneath her skin, and suddenly the forest around me disappears. In its place a rickety wooden dock, weathered by salt spray. A single-masted ship, its sails furled, lists gently at anchor. Beyond, an ancient town crouches behind crumbling stone walls. My breath hitches as a figure steps down the gangplank—Dave; muscles taut beneath a linen shirt, rolling a heavy barrel off the deck.

"I see him," I whisper. "Oh my god, I really see him."

Claudia gently withdraws her arm. "Now we must go to the hawthorn tree," she instructs, pointing to a twisted sapling at the clearing's edge.

"Why?" I ask.

"So, we can speak with him. Back in 1921, I was able to see Marie in 1649, but a hawthorn tree had been imperative to the process. Hawthorns are often where the veil between realms is thinnest."

Gordan sidles up, curiosity in his sharp eyes. "Are you journeying to the faerie realm?"

"We're only talking to Dave," Claudia replies coolly, first looking the wrong direction and then correcting herself. Unilateral deafness doesn't allow her to tell the direction of sound. Gordan's pupils widen, then he bows and retreats, leaving us in peace.

Claudia teaches me an incantation as we step beneath the hawthorn's skeletal branches.

"I will draw the moon,
The herb's blessing by the earth;
As long as my will endures,
No distance may divide,
And thus my voice be heard."

Gordan returns, dropping a wicker basket of offerings—strawberries, rosemary sprigs, a silver thimble of honey—into Claudia's hands. "The fae adore tribute," he warns, eyes dancing.

We chant together. The night breeze stirs to life, leaves whispering like a forest chorus. I picture Dave's face, his smile of gentle surprise. In a swirl of pale light he appears, recognition blooming in his eyes. "Orla?" He breathes. "How…?"

Leaves spin around us, suffusing the air with a rustling green glow…and then he vanishes.

"No!" I cry, clutching Claudia's arm. "Where did he go?"

"I'm not sure," she says, unease creasing her brow.

My pulse thunders in my ears until, as if carried on the wind, Dave reappears right in front of me. I rush forward, cradling his face in my hands. "You're back," I sob.

His hand cups my cheek before pulling me into a fierce embrace. "Do I even want to know what spell yanked me here?" he murmurs, kissing my forehead.

Claudia paces behind us. "The incantation was meant only for communication, not transport."

"Then how…?" I start to ask.

Dave's brow furrows. "I felt static…a low vibration…just before everything shifted."

Claudia's eyes narrow. "It's him again, Cromwell. He's manipulating us, treating us like pawns."

At that moment, Marie hurries over. "Gather everyone and bring your tools to the lighthouse tonight," she urges.

Florian bounds up, excitement crackling around her. "Everything's ready for the nuptials!"

As the others disperse, Dave's fingers lace through mine. "Ready to explore the mind of a psychopath?" he teases, voice soft.

"Let's save it for home." I nudge him playfully, though my heart races.

*****

"Ready?" Dave asks in our bedroom, lifting my hand to his forehead as he channels his connection to Cromwell. A stray sunbeam slants through the curtains, illuminating the faint sheen of sweat on his brow.

I press my other palm against his chest, whispering encouragement. Notes of san-

dalwood and cedar cling to us both. I wonder if Cromwell's earlier transportation
forged an even stronger psychic tether with
Dave.

Then Cromwell's thoughts surge
through Dave; not the twisted vengeance I
anticipated, but laughter—a father rejoic-
ing in the embraces of children who have
not been reincarnated. A tender moment,
until his voice booms within our minds.
"My beloved Elizabeth, and our child, be-
long to me. Elizabeth's place is at my side."

No fury, only stark authority. I struggle
to form a question. "What of Ethel? The
people?"

Cromwell snarls back, "You should be
grateful to simply exist. Without me, none
of you would."

And like that, the link severs, not allowing us to gain any useful information. "No,
no, no!" I wail as Dave gathers me close.
His arms are a sanctuary, warm and safe.

After everything that's happened, everything we've been through, I don't want to

think about any of that. I'd rather think about the comfort of being in Dave's strong arms again. Because this might be the last time I'm in them. I bury my face in his chest, drawing strength from the rise and fall of his heartbeat. I press a trembling kiss on his collarbone, tasting salt and reassurance. His hands travel over my back, sliding beneath my shirt, flames of longing flickering between us.

I arch into him as he peels the fabric away, skin meeting skin. In the soft glow of lamplight, every ridge of his torso is sculpted art; broad shoulders, a taut abdomen, the line of his hips disappearing into the waistband of his jeans. Our lips meet again, deeper now, tasting and exploring.

His hands roam my sides, slipping beneath my trousers before gently pulling them down. I release a breathy moan, the sound of it echoing in the quiet room. His mouth follows his hands, nipping at my ear, trailing heat down my neck. When his lips find me where I need him most, I dissolve entirely, each caress sending rivulets of delight through my veins.

He lifts his head, and our eyes lock—an unspoken promise of trust—before he guides himself inside me. Every movement is a conversation of bodies. The press of his chest against mine, the flex of his back muscles, the way my muscles clench and release around him. Waves of euphoria crest as we move together, breath mingling, hearts pounding in perfect sync, until there is nothing left but the electric bond forged in love and need.

CHAPTER THIRTEEN—MOLLY
"As you slide down the banisters of life,
may the splinters never point the wrong
way."

As the Samhain festivities begin, Orla and I weave through the crowd and meet back by the old tree stump. I don't even mind that the sun was already approaching setting before she arrived. Her shirt is torn, but she has Dave back, and relief warms me from head to toe. The cool wind rustles dead leaves at our feet; we must recruit reinforcements before midnight's last toll. Thankfully, most of our long-distance friends, as close as kin, gathered here treat our tales like gospel—no questions asked. This festival ground has always felt like home, a reunion of distant hearts tied by magic.

We step side by side onto the muddy path, lantern light flickering against Orla's cheekbones. The smell of burning oak and spiced cider drifts across the clearing, and every drumbeat reverberates in my chest. Memories rise with each footfall; laughter spilling around bonfires, barefoot dances in dew-damp grass. Then a flash of gold catches my eye. I tap Orla's shoulder and point at a woman with a long blonde braid, coiled low, threads of light dancing through its plaits. Her purple bustier, embroidered with silver runes, gleams like an amethyst star. I remember that knowing gaze she cast on us three years ago and wonder how much she knows.

"How are you, Monica?" Orla's voice rings bright over the music.

"Splendid," Monica replies, lifting her chin beneath a wreath of ivy. "My thesis was accepted! How are you two?"

I exhale. "Actually, we came for you. We're in trouble, and your magical intelligence is, frankly, the best we've got."

Monica's brow arches. "What's happening?"

Under the canopy of trees, I explain the ghost that haunts Ethel—how it siphoned

travelers from other worlds into this one—
and how our only victory demands sacrificing Ethel herself. Monica's eyes flicker
with sympathy and alarm.

"Just as the visitors prepare to banish
the spirit," she says, voice firm, "we cloak
Ethel in a ward that blinds the ghost."

"Blinding alone sounds feeble," Orla
counters, concern lacing her words.

Monica nods, lips pressed together. "I
wasn't finished. After cloaking, we bind
extra wards, barriers of salt and starlight, to
repel any spectral breach."

"That sounds good, but the group seems
to think that ending the ghost will simultaneously end Ethel, like they're connected,"
I say, not mentioning that this town is a
counter world created by Cromwell.

She holds up her hand. "Finally, we'll
transfer this world's power to someone we
trust utterly."

"So, you'll help us?" Orla's plea trembles in the lantern glow.

Monica smiles, fidgeting with a loose thread in the embroidery on her bustier. "Meet at the lighthouse? What time?"

"Just before midnight," I say. "You'll be able to enjoy the festivities beforehand."

As Monica drifts away, Orla lifts her voice above the murmur to call Dave. "Dave? Are Claudia and Lina ready? Florian and Kiersten learned the Ulster curse from Claudia, right?"

Dave's voice crackles through the phone. "All set."

"What about Alex and Thomas?" I ask. "Conor and Liam practiced the binding spell with Étaín and Róis?"

"We've got it covered," Dave says. "And you and Cormac?"

I force a laugh. "Yes, absolutely!" I lie, though a sudden metallic ringing pounds inside my skull. The night air turns jagged, each breath sharp as shattered glass.

Orla's eyes widen; she presses a hand to her mouth and mouths, "No!" Then she clasps my forearm, knuckles white. "I need to be sure Dave's okay. The call disconnected."

I nod, voice tight. "And I have to check on Cormac."

*****

Entering the apartment, I'm flooded with relief to see Cormac safe and sound. I rush over and embrace her tightly. "You're alright!"

"Of course, I am," she replies, then notices me touching my ear. "Oh, no!"

"I thought you might be upset with me," I begin. "But we need to work together to overcome this and keep anyone else we care about from dying. I don't think I could handle losing another person."

"I'm not upset with you," she responds. "I just needed some time and space to process everything."

I drop my hands and look down. She lifts my chin with her finger, forcing me to meet her gaze.

"After a lot of thought," she says, inhaling and smiling as my stomach does somersaults. "My answer is yes!"

I pull out the velvet box from my pocket and slip the moonstone ring onto her finger. As I grin in joy, Cormac's lips meet mine in a kiss that quickly turns from sweet to passionate and urgent. Our hands explore each other's bodies. Her mouth on my neck sends a shiver of delight through me. I grab her hips and pull her close; the feeling is exquisite.

Once we reach the bed, Cormac leans over me. Her lips brush against mine before she kisses behind my ear. Her hands run from my hips to the edge of my shirt, making me gasp as her fingertips trace my skin. She removes my shirt and tosses it aside. As we both undress, everything feels perfectly right.

Her hands glide over my lower stomach and down the side of my leg until her fingers brush my inner thigh. She slowly moves her fingers higher, our bare skin pressing together. Before she can continue, I sit up and turn her around so she's sitting in front of me between my legs.

I slip my hand between her legs while lifting her chin with my other hand to kiss her neck. I find the spot that brings her the most pleasure while moving my other hand to her breast. She arches her back in ecstasy. I gently pinch and pull her nipples while moving my other hand in a steady rhythm. I continue to massage her as she presses her pelvis against my palm. Our breathing becomes ragged until she reaches her climax.

Then she turns back around, pulling me down to lie beside her again. Her hands move to my thighs, parting them as her mouth travels. She expertly sucks and licks while my head spins. As she continues, I feel a radiating warmth at my core. Her hand softly moves over my hardened nipple while the thumb of her other hand massages my clit. My head arches back as I feel it building, closer and closer until I scream out her name as she brings me to completion.

We hold each other tightly but then glance at the clock—it's time! Rapidly, we gather our things and depart as I wonder if I should call anybody to warn them about the ringing I heard. Did Alex hear it too? Who could it be for? We are heading into battle…and slowly I realize that it could be for anyone.

*****

A tight cluster of visitors presses around the lighthouse. Claudia and Alex stand beneath Florian's woven arch, their hands touching. Lina hovers at Claudia's elbow; Thomas braces himself beside Alex. Marie grips her officiant's script. Elizabeth ushers Étaín and Róis toward the lighthouse, horseshoes clenched in their fists; the boy's ruffled collar folded like a silent prayer. We're set the moment midnight's bell tolls.

A chill fog slithers ashore, curling around our ankles, and without a word the bonfire roars to life, flames blazing gold against the darkness as if Cromwell's malignant will fuels it. From one of the boats come soft, measured footfalls. Cormac and I snap into fighting stances, hearts hammering.

A small figure emerges. The boy. Dirt smudges his cheeks. "How did you get here?" Marie demands, voice trembling.

He glances down, dragging the toe of his shoe through the earth. "I hid on the boat," he whispers.

Before anyone can breathe, a voice booms across the salt wind: "Son!" Cromwell's tone cracks the air like a cannon shot.

I catch Vienna's eye and nod, our silent cue. She floods his mind with visions of every brutal atrocity he wrought at the facility, only now reborn upon his own children. The air vibrates like a shockwave with his anger.

Kiersten springs forward, snatches the boy into her arms, and dissolves into the crowd. Orla edges beside Monica, blocking her from sight as Monica transfers protective wards into the night.

"It's stopped working!" Lina says as she and Claudia hold hands, soul possessing Cromwell.

But before I can unleash Nelly and Olinda's ward, three heavy boots pound the path. And then we see Cromwell and his counters, Ruarc and Aodhán, in the flesh walking toward us. What sorcery is this?

"Where is he?" he roars.

Cormac chants while I look at him. I open my mouth and unleash a shriek so piercing it rattles stones. Cromwell deflects it like a blade, hurling the scream skyward. It slams against the lighthouse wall, showering us with flinching sparks. Then, with a harsh gesture, he hurls us aside. We slam into jagged rocks ten feet away, blood trickling from torn flesh. Alex and Thomas rush to strike, only to be flung back in a gout of power.

Austria and Josh sprint in. Josh lunges with desperate fury, but Cromwell's hand flicks, and Josh vanishes in a heartbeat. Austria keels over, shrieking. Aodhán binds her wrists in rough rope.

Marie presses the vow scroll to Claudia and Alex. Their voices ring out as Florian scatters lavender-scented rope rings into their palms. In one sweeping move, Claudia tosses something small—an obsidian shard possibly—into Florian's swirling dance. Florian spins toward Cromwell and thrusts a dagger with merciless precision.

Cromwell bats it aside; the blade clatters to stone, nicking his palm. Ruarc lunges to bind Florian in hemp, but Kiersten crashes into him, hurling her ax home. It buries itself in his chest. Ruarc's roar rips the night as he collapses. Aodhán falls with him as if they're linked. Florian tumbles into Kiersten's arms, tears and relief mingling on her cheeks.

"I only want Elizabeth and the boy!" Cromwell bellows at Ruarc's crumpled form.

At that moment, Elizabeth steps from the lighthouse, Étaín and Róis burying the relics behind her feet. "No," she cries, voice absolute. "The curse is broken. You must go."

Claudia and Alex edge to the blazing pit and hurl their lavender rings into the heart of the flame. In perfect harmony they intone, "Leave this world, Cromwell. You are not welcome here."

Cromwell's lips curl into a slow, defiant smirk instead of dissolving into dust as he did three years past. The lighthouse beacon sweeps across his face, a cruel reminder of that desperate Mayday call. "If I can't have what I love, neither can you!" He bellows. Simultaneously, Dave and Cormac collapse, clutching their throats in silent agony.

Gordan steps forward beside Vienna, his eyes cold with purpose—he's learned to starve souls dry rather than feed them.

Cromwell levels his hand at Vienna. Yesha steps forward, then bursts into feathers and takes flight as a crow. Cromwell looses magical arrow after arrow, but she weaves through the shafts with uncanny grace. As she dips toward him, his pupils balloon. With a single, bloody plunge, she dives into his chest—leaving only a scattering of black feathers drifting down.

Cromwell's scream tears the night, then vanishes. Where once his figure stood, only a wisp of shadow evaporates into the fog. Gordan lowers his head. "She led him to his final death," he intones softly. "I stand as watcher at the guarding of his end. May Morrigan be."

CHAPTER FOURTEEN—ORLA

"May the Irish hills caress you.
May her lakes and rivers bless you.
May the luck of the Irish enfold you.
May the blessings of Saint Patrick behold
you."

Everyone collapses into a tight cluster; limbs tangled in a collective embrace. The air vibrates with a heady mix of triumph and stunned relief, as if the world itself is exhaling.

"I can't believe he's finally gone after generations of torment," Claudia murmurs, her voice quivering.

"Yes," Marie replies, brushing dust from her sleeves. "He's gone. Is everyone all right?"

Alex flexes his fingers, revealing faint scraps of torn fabric and shallow cuts. "Just a few scratches."

"I'm not!" Vienna's voice cracks as her bonds fall away, and she bursts free like a bird shaken from its nest. "Yesha… she, she turned to feathers."

Gordan steps forward, his shoes thudding softly on the grass. He lowers his voice to a gentle rumble. "She never recovered from Cromwell slaying her brother. In her grief, she made a pact with the Goddess Morrigan, sacrificing herself to gain the power to avenge him."

"No," Vienna spits into the dusk, eyes blazing. "She loved Barren. She wouldn't abandon him that easily."

Gordan rests a hand on her shaking shoulder. "Barren understood her choice. You know she isn't truly gone; through Morrigan, she lives on in every whisper of wind, every rustle of leaves, across every world and every age."

Sierra, her features an uncanny mirror of Vienna's, falls into step beside her. She drapes an arm around Vienna's trembling shoulders. "I bet Vex can find a way to speak with Yesha again."

A ripple of relief courses through the group. The visitors didn't vanish with Cromwell's death, as they predicted, and I allow myself a private smile. After all, Monica entrusted me with the stewardship of this world. "Shall we proceed?" I ask, voice warm.

Vienna inhales, forcing a small, brave smile. "Anything to shift my mind from heartbreak."

Cormac carefully unfolds a portable keyboard, its ivory keys catching the last pale light of evening, and hands it to Kiersten, who is already perched on a wooden crate. Then Cormac retrieves her guitar from the boat's stern and tunes each string until its silver twang rings clear. When they begin their gentle counterpoint, with Cormac's guitar weaving arpeggios around Kiersten's rolling chords, I feel goosebumps rise along my arms.

As Vienna and Al step beneath the wooden arch, its branches whipped into curling vines; I summon the vision. A small clopil perches beyond the arch and emits a bright beep. Two kindly doctors in starched white coats wave from the other side, their identification badges swinging. Beside them, a large colorful parrot tilts its head and fusses with the hem of one doctor's lapel.

Tears spring to Vienna's eyes as the portal's light washes over faces she has missed. Sierra and Marrit burst forward hand in hand, sprinting toward a tall man with charcoal eyes, Yesha's partner Barren. One by one, travelers rush through the shimmering threshold and fade from view, reappearing in their home world to embrace loved ones beneath a glowing sunset.

Molly's voice trembles behind me. "Will they be all right?"

I remind her of the crystal ball in the clearing where Nelly left it. "We'll monitor them from that."

Dave folds me into a side hug, a teasing glint in his eye. "You had a hand in this, didn't you?"

When the last figure from their group steps through, the arch glow dims. But in my mind's eye, I see each reunion: laughter, tears, relief.

Next, Austria and her crew get in line, faces streaked with sweat and joy. Austria's eyes, still red-rimmed, shine brighter than any star when she sees Josh waiting beyond the portal. His rowdy team hollers and slaps Josh on the back as if to say, "We told you she'd be fine." Then they vanish in a swirl of golden light. I feel the sudden emptiness settle in my chest.

Elizabeth, Étaín, Róis, and Neasa amble forward, teasing one another like siblings. Their laughter drifts back to me, warm and familiar. My gaze lands on Molly, and my heart warms.

A rebuilt Drogheda shimmers into view: sturdy walls in front of crimson rooftops under a lavender sky. Standing at its gates are Mary and Barnabus, flanked by two red-haired women whose fingertips cradle blooms of pink firewood wildflower.

The blossoms pulse with untamed, ancient magic, petals drifting like embers in the breeze. As Elizabeth's party steps through, her young son turns, grins, and waves—a silent farewell that tugs at my soul.

Finally, Claudia and Alex share a gentle, rain-soft kiss beneath the arch. One by one, the remaining visitors from the 1920s follow them into a swirling Jazz Age of smoky clubs and fresh fights for equality. The portal snaps shut, leaving us bathed in the moonlight's shimmer.

We gather again, this time in a quieter embrace, savoring the intimate calm. Together, we collect stray ribbons, stack folding chairs, and sweep away footprints in the dirt. Somewhere, Cromwell's dark influence, along with Ruarc's and Aodhán's bodies, has dissolved into nothingness.

Cormac brushes a loose strand of hair from Molly's face and grins at me. "Has Molly told you?"

I arch an eyebrow.

She holds up a pale moonstone ring that glows softly in the sheen of the waxing gibbous. "I said yes."

I leap forward, sweeping both Molly and Cormac into a jubilant hug. "Dave, we absolutely must throw an engagement party."

He flashes me a thumbs-up with one hand, the other balancing four stacked chairs on his shoulder, and laughs. The promise of celebration rings through the night, bright as any portal's glow.

*****

Under a softly dappled canopy of lavender wisteria, several picnic tables stand nestled among mossy roots in the quiet wood. Cascading clusters of blossoms hang like delicate chandeliers, and between them tiny faerie lights, small orbs of warm glow, twinkle as if fireflies had taken permanent residence. The tables are dressed in crisp white linens edged with lilac trim; each place setting glints with polished silverware, fine China plates painted in floral motifs, and crystal goblets that catch the light. A faint breeze stirs the petals, carrying the floral perfume of wisteria. Now all we need is the happy couple.

"Come take a look at what Ben has set up," Dave murmurs to me, his hand sliding gently into mine.

We follow the winding path of sunlit earth and see the same circular table Nelly used at Samhain. Tonight, it's dressed in a fitted ivory cloth tied with a sumptuous purple bow. At its center rests Nelly's crystal ball, translucent and shimmering with inner light.

"I think I've figured out how to use it," Ben says, voice low with excitement.

"He can do absolutely anything," Kyle teases, draping an arm around Ben's shoulders. "That is, when he puts his mind to it."

Ben smacks his chest in mock pride, and their laughter—bright and easy— warms my heart.

"Shall we?" Ben invites, tilting his head toward the crystal sphere.

"Let's wait for Molly," I reply.

Just then, Molly appears, bearing four flutes of pale-gold champagne; Cormac follows with two more. She winks at me; her cheeks flushed with joy.

"I know what you're going to say next," Dave teases Molly. "That some of us know how to keep a woman happily in bed."

We all chuckle and raise our glasses before leaning in to watch the crystal ball's surface swirl and glow. Beyond us, friends dance beneath the hanging blooms, laughter mingling with the twinkling lights. This is a perfect engagement party for Molly and Cormac.

Ben waves a hand above the ball, and an image materializes: Austria's world. Stone arches and marble columns surround a museum café; a fountain bubbles at the center, its spray catching light. Austria sits with Josh and others, plates of steaming soup and crusty bread before them. Tiffany and Luke share a booth at the edge; their hands entwined, foreheads touching.

"So, are you guys ready to scare people again?" Ceresa asks, her eyes shining with anticipation.

"I'm just glad altered helixes no longer need a serum for protection," Jack, a younger guy with curls brushing his temple, says. "Now that they're no longer being hunted by Cromwell's reincarnated soul."

"And there's no longer a need for another world since our environment is healing," a woman with silver-streaked hair, old enough to be Austria's mother, adds gently. Beside her, a man who could be her father nods, a proud smile on his face. There's also a sweet elderly woman with cookies sitting by them.

"I have my family back!" Austria breathes, tears glinting at the corners of her eyes. We all applaud, voices echoing through the woodland canopy.

Ben gestures again, and the crystal ball shifts to Vienna's world: the interior of a gleaming spaceship; smooth metal corridors lit by pulsing blue lines. Al and Vienna float in zero gravity, laughter bubbling from their lips.

"Glad to be back traveling the universe!" Al says, looping an arm around Vienna's waist.

"Where would you like to go first, Barren?" Vienna asks the young man with charcoal eyes at her side.

"You mentioned Planet Forset is mostly animals and non-human inhabitants, right?" Barren inquires.

"Yeah, we're actually really close," Al replies as Vex, their little clopil robot, rolls up beside them with cheerful beeps. "I can confirm that is where you'll be closer to Yesha," Vex chimes.

They land on a lush world of emerald forests. Even from here, I can almost feel the warm humidity and hear distant calls of strange creatures. Tears glisten in my eyes. A sleek crow swoops down and perches on Barren's shoulder, its feathers shimmering. We all have tears in our eyes with that.

Next, we find ourselves in the 1920s: Claudia, Alex, and friends seated around a table adorned with lace and an oil lamp's soft glow. Olinda places a steaming roast at the center; Marie, Anna, and Nelly clap. Frank, James, and Thomas rise together to carve.

"We're putting together a rally," Florian announces, her voice firm.

"That's right!" Kiersten adds, adjusting the cloche hat atop her head. "Women have the right to vote, but there should be federal funding for maternal health."

"Yeah, let's end the male bias in the medical field!" Lina adds.

Frank and Thomas place hands over their hearts; Alex lays his palm gently on Claudia's pregnant belly. Molly murmurs, "Still fighting the good fight," and we applause anew.

Finally, the scene shifts to 1649: a rustic dwelling warmed by a crackling yule log. Elizabeth, Étaín, Róis, Mary, and Barnabus feast on hearty stew and spiced bread. Outside, mist swirls under the pale moonlight.

"They arrived on flying ships through the mist," Barnabus begins. "Skilled in the arts and Druidry, they embodied divine order and knowledge."

"I do love these tales!" Róis exclaims before Étaín hushes her with a playful finger to the lips.

"When humans drove them back, they retreated into the sídhe, becoming the fae we know today, Aos Sí. If they carry a human to their realm, a short visit can mean centuries have passed when they return."

The image fades, and I find myself thinking of Étaín's old legend: a fae queen reborn as a human butterfly. I shake off the reverie and look around at my friends.

"I say we toast our visitors," Molly declares, lifting her glass.

"May they enjoy the rest of their lives," Cormac adds.

"May their fights for equality be successful," Kyle calls.

"Ditto!" Ben grins at him.

"May all of us never face an evil like Cromwell again!" Dave exclaims.

"I would like to toast the happily engaged couple," I conclude.

Glasses clink, and we sip the champagne; the golden bubbles sweet on our tongues. As I lower my flute, a delicate butterfly, its wings painted like stained glass, alights on the rim. A smile spreads across my face. Dave's lips meet mine, and in the soft warmth of his kiss, I melt into pure delight.

THE END OF THE ENCHANTED TRAVELERS UNIVERSE

ACKNOWLEDGMENTS

Much thanks to Kelly Allenby, Kerry Topping, Amy Brewer, and Giselle Depres who graciously helped me improve and highlight the final book in the Enchanted Travelers universe. They caught things I'd missed, helped me improve wording, and reignited my love of writing. Gratitude also to the ICU staff who saved me. While I continue to suffer from 90 dB tinnitus 24/7 because of the illness, they did save my life and for that I will be ever grateful. And now you know where my inspiration for Molly's power comes from.

More thanks to my fellow Stacked Book Club members. You always bring new books to my attention, keeping my reading fresh. Smart and conversational, they also happen to be some of my favorite dinner companions. Finally, love and appreciation to my family and close friends for supporting me and putting up with my chaotic book habits.

ABOUT THE AUTHOR

Stephanie Hansen is a PenCraft and Global Book Award Winning Author. Her debut novella series, *Altered Helix*, released in 2020. It hit the #1 New Release, #1 Best Seller, and other top 100 lists on Amazon. It is now being adapted to an animated story for Tales. Her debut novel, *Replaced Parts*, released in 2021 through Fire & Ice YA and Tantor Audio. It has been in a Forbes article, hit Amazon bestseller lists, and made the Apple young adult coming soon bestsellers list. The second book in the Transformed Nexus series, *Omitted Pieces*, released in 2022. Her debut paranormal romance, *Ghostly Howls*, released in 2023. Her debut historical romantasy, *Armored Hours*, released in 2024. It's sequel, *Guarded Time*, released in 2025. She is a member of the deaf and hard of hearing community, so she tries to incorporate that into her fiction. https://www.authorstephaniehansen.com/

HTTPS://WWW.AUTHORSTEPHANIEHANSEN.COM/